BLiSS
UNCOVERED

A double life - a single truth.

TONY J FORDER

A DI Bliss Prequel Novella

tonyjforder.com
tony@tonyjforder.com

Also by Tony J Forder

The DI Bliss Series
Bad to the Bone
The Scent of Guilt
If Fear Wins
The Reach of Shadows
The Death of Justice
Endless Silent Scream
Slow Slicing

The Mike Lynch Series
Scream Blue Murder
Cold Winter Sun

Standalones
Degrees of Darkness
Fifteen Coffins

To those who inspired me,
and to those who inspire me still.

ONE

LLUMINATED BY A STRIP of spotlights suspended by dusty chains hanging from a high ceiling, John, Paul, George and Ringo huddled together around a pool table. Its canvas cover had been left on and stretched tight to protect the cloth, forming a solid platform upon which John had spread out two large paper items.

The first was a map of Edmonton, north London, which had circles of red ink drawn over a trading park by the Angel Road railway station, in addition to two separate locations along the beige line indicating the A406 North Circular Road. The second item was an unrolled set of blueprints, now being kept flat by pool cues placed at each end.

Other than the four men, the snooker hall was quiet and empty. The pool table was one of four standing at the back of the cavernous room on the first floor, up the single rise of a creaky wooden stairway likely to fail any stringent Health and Safety inspection. Paul managed the business, and had turfed out the last pair of customers at midnight, promising them two free games of snooker as he put a halt to the one they were drunkenly labouring over. The four Beatles spoke openly the moment they knew they could not be overheard.

'Walk me through it again,' John said, indicating both the map and blueprints. 'As if we were on the clock this time.'

'How many times do we have to go over it?' Paul complained. 'I'm sick of all this palaver.'

'We do it as often as I say so.' This time when he spoke, John had an edge to his voice. Though it was not aimed at him, George didn't like its cadence one bit. John was unpredictable and liable to flare up at the slightest provocation. He and Paul were always on each other's case, oozing testosterone as their chests puffed out like squabbling roosters. It was a volatile situation, and one he was keen to avoid allowing to disintegrate any further.

'I think we're meant to go over it until it becomes second nature,' he said, looking between the two quarrelling men. He thought it best to offer each of them a bone. 'I can understand why you're pissed off with going over it again and again, Paul, but it's better to be overcooked than raw.'

Seemingly placated, both John and Paul nodded in agreement. They all looked to Ringo, who flashed a mischievous grin and got into it. 'All right, chaps. Rely on the drummer to hold the beat. By the time we're a go, I've already planted my device a couple of days prior, and it's set to trigger at 6.20pm precisely. That'll set off the fire alarm and activate the sprinklers within ten minutes at the outside. We're already on the move when it all kicks off, and I give it enough time for the evacuation of the building to begin before calling the fire service mobilising unit and cancelling the shout. I have the store security code, so they'll regard it as legit and turn the appliances back.'

'I take us off the North Circular here,' George said, stabbing a finger at one of the red circles. 'We enter the industrial park and I pull up behind the warehouse by the loading bay.'

Ringo nodded. 'With John and Paul hidden away in the back of the van, I have a word with the manager and tell him we have to run a check in case the alarm device is faulty, make sure there isn't anything smouldering, before giving them the all-clear to return.'

As one, the four of them hunched over the blueprint. 'Once inside,' John said, 'Ringo makes safe his device and bags it up to take with us when we leave. Paul accesses the alarm system, deactivates the automatic door closing feature and the alarms, and centrally unlocks all the doors for us. We make our way into the room behind the manager's office where they keep the safe. Next…?'

'I'm up,' George said quickly. 'I get the safe open while you three spread wide the holdalls we brought with us.'

John nodded. 'On the way out, you tell the manager you've cleared the place and reset the codes, so he should give it ten minutes before trying to access the building again.'

'Before leaving the estate, we pull over to strip off the livery and decals and dump them. We also toss the fake plates. Then I follow the route out and enter the North Circular at the second red mark on the map. I then hover around the speed limit until we reach our two getaway motors.'

John stood upright, folded his arms and surveyed both documents. He was a brute of a man, with massive arms wrapped across a huge chest. The kind of man it might take dynamite to put down. 'Ringo, how soon are you going to have the livery for the van?'

By contrast, Ringo was the smallest of them. A wiry little character who popped and fizzed like unstable electricity, unable to stand still and always bobbing his head to a beat only he could hear. 'I'm getting each part made up at a different printing shop, and I'm expecting the last of them by the end of the week.'

'Good idea that, spreading the work. George, what's your plan for the two getaway motors?'

'I don't want to nick them too early. The longer I have them, the more risk I take. So, soon as you decide on the day we're taking this place down, I'll go out and find us our cars. I'll make sure I have them purring and set up in place the night before. Ringo is going to give me a hand with them.'

'And the safe?' John asked. 'Still no concerns there?'

'None at all. I know that Chubb model inside out. You wouldn't believe how many people forget to change the combination from the factory default, most of which are known. I'll give them a try first, but I'll get it open either way. No worries.'

After a few seconds, John stepped back from the table. 'I think we're just about there. Ringo, you give me the nod when the last of the livery decals are ready. The van is being sprayed as we speak. That's costing us a monkey, but I think we can spare it if that safe is bulging like I expect it to be.'

George nodded. 'We all know our roles, and this is starting to feel good. How about we forget all this Beatles malarkey for once, and introduce ourselves properly? John, you pulled this crew together, so you kick off.'

'Fair play to you, Georgie boy. Just for now, mind. After tonight, we're back to our Fab Four. Lads… I'm Declan O'Shea.'

'Dermot O'Shea's brother,' Paul said, grinning. Physically, he had approximately the same stamp as George, but sported a full beard and walked with a slight limp and a skip that suggested he had once worn a calliper to correct something in the leg.

'The one and only. He's the silent partner I mentioned before. The man who gave us our in at the warehouse, the layout, alarm codes, recall code, and the expected time of the armoured car collection. He also has the connection to the man in charge.'

'Then he's more than worth his cut,' Paul said.

O'Shea grinned. 'And your man, Paul, here goes by the name of Roy Gilbert. I know that because my brother threw his name into the ring first because of his alarms and electrics speciality. We've known each other for a wee while, but this is our first job together.'

The man they knew as Paul grinned. 'Yeah, that's me. So who's our fireman?' he asked, looking over at Ringo.

The man with the easy grin said, 'My name's Billy Knowles.'

The three turned to George. 'And you, Peterman?' John asked.

George knew the term "Peterman" was another word for a safecracker, though the origins of the phrase were muddy. He nodded around the table. 'Good to meet you all formally, gents. My name is Vincent Styles,' said Jimmy Bliss.

TWO

FRIDAY NIGHT IN THE Bliss household had been fish and chips night for as long as Jimmy could remember. He wasn't a great fan of fish, so he usually opted for a breast of roast chicken or a pie, occasionally a couple of sausages in batter. But whenever duty allowed, the entire family – such as it was – sat at the dining table dead on 6.30pm and ate straight out of the paper wrappers.

Jimmy was at peace with himself. He'd been dating Hazel Smith for approaching eleven months now, and as far as he could recall, she had missed only a couple of Friday night dinners during that time. His girlfriend came from a relatively affluent family. When she spoke, her correct pronunciation lacking any obvious accent stuck out like handlebars on a giraffe. She dressed stylishly, her clothes elegant and expensive. Yet for all this, she had seamlessly integrated into the working-class Bliss family as if she had always belonged. Marriage had not yet been discussed, yet both Dennis and Jacqui Bliss treated Hazel as if she had already taken their son's name. Jimmy loved that about his parents, and he adored his girlfriend for making it so easy for them to love her, too.

'You two off to the pictures tonight?' his mum asked, looking between the couple. She carved her way through a piece of skate; her favourite.

'Might as well,' Jimmy said, stifling a yawn. 'We ain't going to find anything as good as that *Prime Suspect* on the telly for a good while.'

Dennis Bliss started to choke on his cod. He cleared his throat and took a swig from a bottle of London Pride ale. 'As if the force is still like that towards women,' he said, shaking his head to amplify his irritation with the show. 'I'm not saying sexism doesn't still exist in the job, but they went too far with it. Mind you, that Helen Mirren is a bit of a sort.'

'Oi!' Jacqui wagged her fork in his direction. 'Keep your mincers off her. Not that I should worry. She'd swallow you whole and spit you out in bubbles.'

The dining room echoed to their laughter. When it quietened down, Hazel regarded Jimmy and said, 'I don't mind going to the cinema again if there's something good on.'

'I'll have a look in the paper after dinner. Anything you fancy in particular, Haze?'

Hazel shook her head. Put a hand over her mouth while she finished chewing. 'I have no idea what's out. *Silence of the Lambs* is coming shortly, and we must see that. I enjoyed the book so much.'

'Who's in that one?' Dennis asked.

'Anthony Hopkins and Jodie Foster.'

'Hmm. Another sort.'

This time his remark earned him a slapped arm, which got them laughing again. Pushing her folded wrappings to one side, Jacqui turned to Hazel. 'Been working on anything big lately, love?'

Hazel nodded enthusiastically. Her full cheeks rounded further and shone beneath the dining room lights. 'I'm heading up a campaign for a major company called Apple. They're releasing their version of the notebook.'

Jimmy clocked the lines deepen on his mother's forehead. He chuckled. 'No, not the kind of notebook you're thinking of, Mum. It's what they call a miniaturised computer, one that's small enough to sit on your lap if you want it to.'

His mother appeared no less bemused. 'So where does the... you know, the screen thingamabob go?'

'It's built in, Jacqui,' Hazel answered. 'It flips open like a lid, using hinges. The units themselves are extremely heavy, and mostly for business use still. But these people at Apple are predicting that most homes will have one within the next decade.'

'They have us using computers at the front desk these days,' Dennis said, as if affronted by the idea. 'I just got used to the bleeding things when they tell me we're going to move to a different type of system. They say all the menus will be taken away, and instead we'll see all kinds of graphics or some such on the screen. Sounds bloody crazy if you ask me.'

'It's the future, Dennis,' Hazel said. 'People like IBM and Apple are making a small fortune out of it. And there's a company – another American one, of course – called Microsoft that's causing a real stir in the tech industry.'

'I don't know what the world is coming to. Computers doing the jobs it once took whole offices full of people to do, phones that you can carry around with you, shiny silver discs replacing my old albums and cassettes... it doesn't bear thinking about how quickly things are changing.'

Jimmy sat back, listening and smiling to himself. By no stretch of the imagination were his parents elderly to his mind, but they were an aphorism when it came to dwelling in the past. For his mother, you did not visit the cinema to see a film or movie, you went to the "pictures". As for his father's ancient coffin-like Phillips radiogram currently taking up some major square footage in the living room, when the old man turned that dial to find a sharp signal he was only ever retuning the "wireless", never the radio.

The house was the same. It was the home Jimmy had grown up in. Once every ten years the exterior wood and sills received a fresh coat of paint, because they were exposed to the elements. Inside it was very different. Jimmy had painted over the anaglypta wallpaper himself whenever he fancied a change of colour in his room, but the patterned wallpaper throughout the rest of the house hadn't been replaced in as long as he could remember. His parents had old-fashioned values, spending money on necessities rather than frivolous redecoration.

Bliss loved his parents dearly. They were his world, and he theirs. They'd lost a daughter before she left the womb, eleven months after Jimmy was born. Subsequent complications meant his mother could not conceive again. His father earned a steady living as a uniformed police sergeant, while his mother worked part-time at the nearby Bass Charrington's brewery, both during production and after it had ceased and become the head office. They never had a great deal to spare, but what they did have they lavished on him as often as they could. Every summer the three of them packed up and went somewhere for two weeks, though never abroad. His mother was fascinated by myths and legend, and often they would visit historical landmarks. Wiltshire, with its standing stones, chalk figures and ley lines, had often been a lure. The wide-open spaces and clean air were more than enough of a break for his parents, and Jimmy called upon those fond memories whenever he needed cheering up.

'You going to the Bridge tomorrow, boy?' his father asked.

'Of course.'

'Liverpool will wipe the floor with your lot. You want to support a decent team like the Irons.'

Bliss smiled at the familiar refrain. Born and raised close to the West Ham United football ground, and with a fanatical supporter for a father, it had come as a shock to everyone when at seven, Jimmy had declared his love for Chelsea. To his dad, south-west London might as well have been on the other side of the world, and although their rivalry since had never been aggressive, at times it had become heated. He'd had to put up with it at school as well, where the disagreements often ended in physical confrontations.

'The one thing my team can be relied upon for is to be unreliable,' he said. 'How often do we win the games we ought to lose, only to fu… stuff up the ones we ought to walk?'

'Just don't go getting into any trouble,' his mother warned, frowning at him. 'I know what you're like with your football.'

Bliss rolled his eyes. 'Those days are long gone, mum. There are no proper fights either inside or out-side the grounds anymore. And if one kicks off, I'll turn the other cheek, all right?'

'Well, you be sure you do.'

After dinner, he and Hazel decided against the cinema. Instead they went for a walk, the couple keen to discuss their future in private. Hazel's parents were divorced, and something about their shaky relation-ship had deeply affected her. She was adamant that she and Bliss live together for a while before commit-ting to anything formal, and he had recently started looking around for flats to rent. Unlike his father, who worked at the station closest to the family's terraced house, Jimmy was all for moving out of the area. He had grown up with the kind of conflicts that could arise when a copper policed his own neighbourhood, and wanted no part of that small world. His home life had to be entirely separate from his work, and that was a decision he remained firm about. Hazel's office was in the city, close to Bayswater, and she was perfectly happy to continue using public transport.

'Are you sure you want to do this at all?' Hazel asked him as they walked arm in arm through St Bartholemew's gardens. 'Live together, I mean.'

'Of course. I knew I wanted to spend the rest of my life with you before we'd had our second date.'

'Really?' Her smile melted him all the more. 'It took me a lot longer to reach that point.'

Bliss chuckled. Hazel was beautiful, lithe and energetic, but he admired her honesty most of all. 'That's because I'm a hard bloke to get to know, and therefore a hard bloke to like. But if people can get past that, they see I have certain qualities.'

'No, you're easy to like, Jimmy. It does take a while to get to know the real you under all those layers of protection you have, but it's worth persevering with. I liked you long before I understood you. I loved you before I knew the real you.'

'I'm not sure what any of that means. As far as I know, the real me is what's out there every day. I don't have any front, Haze. With me, what you see is what you get.'

Hazel nodded and hooked her arm tighter around his. 'That's true as far as it goes. No airs, no graces. Just a funny, kind, and loyal man. But you also have hidden depths, and they are polar opposites.'

'How d'you mean?'

'It's like there's the day-to-day you in the middle, the bloke everybody sees and likes and respects. The jovial, gregarious fellow who is always the centre of attention without inviting it. But the reality is that, on the one side there's the hard, intractable and volatile Jimmy, while right at the opposite end of the spectrum you can also find a softer, gentle soul who has empathy leaking out of his pores.'

He stopped walking. Turned to face her. Wrestled his arm free and wrapped both around her. Nose to nose he said, 'I think you make me out to be too complex a person at times, Haze. You see too much, more than is actually there. I can't help wondering if you do that because what I really am is not enough for you.'

Her eyes bored into his. 'Is that why you've been reluctant to find us a place? Because you're not sure about my feelings for you?'

Bliss dipped his head for a moment, before raising it again. 'I can't help but wonder if you're seeing things in me that don't exist, and that when you see me clearly for the first time, you won't like what you find.'

Hazel put a hand to her chest and shook her head. 'If either of us ought to be wary of being found out, Jimmy, it's me. I mean, when we first met you had me down as a straight-laced Catholic girl, all prim and proper. That notion lasted as long as it took you to get me into bed, which was what… two weeks into our relationship. And

I could tell from the look on your face that I took you by surprise that night. And the night after, and possibly every night since. I am that butter wouldn't melt, prissy little thing you can take home to meet your mum and dad. But it's superficial. Deep down, I'm something quite different. I'm unpredictable, and perhaps a little bit crazy. So now who do you think ought to be worrying about the reality of us living together?'

He cupped his hands around her face. 'But don't you see, that's exactly what I love about you? Wherever we go, whoever we run across, you charm them all. Mum and dad adore you, Haze, and my mates have fallen under your spell. To have only that in my life would be all I could wish for. But when we're alone, it's as if you come alive in a completely different way, and all that does is make me love you more.'

Nudging him with her elbow and casting a downward glance, Hazel said, 'So why are we debating this? We both love both sides of the other, and that has to be a rare thing. Jimmy, if you don't find us somewhere soon, I will. It's your birthday next Thursday, and that has to be a turning point. By the end of the month, I want us to have put a deposit down on a nice little flat. I don't care where, but I do care when. You have twenty-eight days by my reckoning. And if you need something else to spur you on, think about how I might treat you on our first night together in our own bed in our own place.'

Bliss swallowed. 'Bugger the end of the month,' he said. 'If I ain't got us a place by the end of next week, you have my permission to spank me.'

Hazel raised her eyebrows. 'Spoilsport,' she said. 'How did you know what your treat was going to be?'

THREE

THE WEEKEND CAME AND went in a bit of a blur. Bliss had two whole days off shift, and he made the most of it. On Saturday he slept in late, and after a quick bowl of cereal got ready and headed across London, tubing it to Fulham Broadway. A couple of pregame pints in the *Cock and Hen*, a few more afterwards in the *Jolly Maltster*. In between, a game beyond all expectations, with the Blues running out winners by four goals to two. The pub was bouncing afterwards right through until around eight, by which time the queues outside the station were gone and Bliss felt the buzz all the way home.

His father had missed his team's game at Charlton because of work, so the following morning after a decent fry-up, the pair went over to Hackney Marshes together to watch some Sunday morning league football. At its peak, the marshes could host over two

and a half thousand players on its one hundred and
twenty pitches, a hive of footballing activity unrivalled
in the whole of the country. With the season over for
many leagues, there were barely a dozen or so games
to choose from, so Jimmy and his father moved on a
couple of times before settling on one that looked lively
enough.

They talked as they watched, the only taboo subject
being their jobs. Long before Jimmy had made his way
out of training at Hendon, his dad had counselled him
on how to strike the right balance between work and
home. Dennis Bliss had witnessed most of the ugli-
est things human beings were capable of doing to one
another, but having never left uniform, his involve-
ment often ended when a case was passed onwards or
upwards. Jimmy had always seen himself as a detective,
and therefore had steeled himself to take on aspects his
father had never experienced – such as seeing a serious
crime investigation through to its bitter conclusion.

His father had thought ahead, and long before
Jimmy set the blue uniform aside, Dennis had introduced him to some hardened, grizzled old detectives
whose lives had been touched by the true horror that
lies in the darkest corners of the human psyche. Men
who'd also been responsible for making sure the mon-
sters who committed those vile crimes paid for it with
jail time.

Not me, Jimmy had told himself at the time. *I'm not going to end up like these men. I'm going to switch myself on when I enter my nick and off again when I leave, because this kind of experience can never, ever enter the home I'm going to make with somebody else.*

Bliss had always regarded his father as an uncomplicated man. An officer whose ambitions were limited, he believed in accountability, and did not shirk his own. Loyal and forthright in his opinions, Dennis Bliss took each day as it came and dealt with the peaks and the troughs as if they were the same. Supporting Chelsea Football Club wasn't the only thing that had drawn Jimmy into fights at school, but he had vowed always to defend his father's honour. Being on the receiving end of an occasional hiding from those who regarded the police with disdain was a price he was willing to pay.

His pugnacious attitude was one of the reasons he had joined a boxing gym at the age of nine. There he learned about discipline and how to protect himself when that self-restraint broke down. At the gym, in and around school, and out on the streets, Bliss had also learned how to cope with temptation. Hand on heart he could never say he'd not been involved in minor misdeeds, but he had learned early on where to draw the line. As his father had before him.

'You miss playing?' his father said to him at one point as the game they were watching became a real thriller.

Having to stop competing in all sports had hit Jimmy early and hit him hard. Damage to the ligaments in his right ankle had initially hampered him when exerting the foot, but increasingly the after-effects led to the swelling making it virtually impossible for him to walk for a good twenty-four hours following a game or a few rounds in the ring. Eventually it came to a straight choice between continuing with his sports or being able to work, and there was only ever going to be one winner.

'I do,' he said, nodding towards the pitch. 'I see some of them a good decade older than me out there and still putting in ninety minutes, getting that rush out of it on a Sunday morning. So, yeah. I miss it like mad.'

'No regrets, though, eh?'

Bliss felt his father's eyes on him now; never an easy load to bear. He shook his head. 'None whatsoever. I miss this, miss pulling on the gloves, but I'm doing a job I enjoy and always knew that was where my real future lay.'

'You have a good head on your shoulders, boy. I always thought you were better in the ring than on a football pitch, but neither of them were ever going to be more than recreational, with a bit of competition along the way.'

'You mean I wasn't good enough to have made a living out of either of them?'

'A little bit, maybe, from the boxing. But not enough to risk having your block knocked off, no.'

An honest man, his father.

After a quick pint, it was back home for the roast – another tradition. Bliss was happy to see Hazel there helping his mother out when they arrived, a ritual she had decided for herself to join in with shortly after the turn of the new year. It had surprised him; Hazel was a modern woman with a full-time executive job and a mindset that refused to accept the role seemingly set aside for women. He had never attempted to convince her otherwise, though he remained a lousy cook who would opt for a sandwich or a bowl of cereal over anything that needed time spent preparing and getting the timing right with hobs and ovens and grills. But Hazel had wanted to fit in with his family, and did not seem to mind this specific role at this specific time.

After dinner, Jimmy washed the dishes and his father dried up and made them all a hot drink. As he sat there nursing his tea, someone on the TV talking about the previous night's Eurovision Song Contest won by Sweden, he glanced around with a smile teasing his lips. A high-flying advertising exec, a Detective Constable, a Police Sergeant, and a home maker and part-time office worker. Theirs was such an ordinary life in so many ways, yet at times so extraordinary as well. He thought of his parents and their many years of happiness together, and as his gaze fell upon Hazel sitting alongside him, he wanted nothing more for himself.

It was, perhaps, the least he could wish for.

But it was also all he could wish for, too.

FOUR

Jimmy Bliss, newly minted Detective Constable a mere seven weeks earlier, walked into the CID squad room on Monday morning to a chorus of loud whistles, boos and ribald jeering. He met the cacophony of sound with a wide grin and a swagger in his gait as he rubbed his thumb and forefinger of his left hand together. The previous week he had taken many bets on the outcome of the game he was attending at Stamford Bridge. Given the average season Bobby Campbell's boys were having, the Blues were odds on for a hiding against Liverpool. But a Kerry Dixon brace, a Dennis Wise penalty, and a Durie effort had seen off the Scousers. Bliss was due a hefty pay out, and he milked it for all he was worth.

'I'm accepting no cheques and I don't take American Express,' he said as he made his way between the aisles to his own desk in the far corner.

He took off his jacket and wrapped it around the back of his chair. Before he'd had a chance to sit down, a beckoning hand coming out of the DI's office wiped the smile from his face. Bliss huffed a silent grumble and raised a thumb, mouthing that he'd be one minute as he wanted to grab a cup of coffee. Detective Inspector Moody's gesticulations cranked up several notches, so Bliss ignored the call of caffeine.

'Shut the door, Bliss,' Moody said, taking a seat but not offering Jimmy the chair on the other side of the desk. The cluttered office stank of stale sweat heavily disguised by body spray. DI Moody was a large man, prone to heavy sweating and a diet of spicy food. It was an anti-social combination. 'And next time you want your morning coffee, I suggest you get one before you come to work.'

Bliss stood mute, his features betraying nothing of what he was feeling inside. Moody was hardly the most welcoming of bosses, and the way he said Jimmy's surname suggested his life had become anything but bliss when the green and lippy DC with a sergeant for a father had appeared in CID.

'What's the SP on the Beatles?' Moody asked. He picked up his own mug of steaming hot coffee and appeared to take great delight in drinking it down and sighing with pleasure after each sip.

'We're on any time soon,' Bliss said. 'It's going down on a Friday night, that much I do know. All we're waiting for is the van to have its livery taken care of. After that, we're good to go.'

'So it could be this week?'

'I'm pretty sure it will be.'

'You have everything in hand?'

'The getaway cars are in the shed over at Limehouse. The mechanics are working on them today, fitting a hidden cut-off switch so that after we've driven them into place I can quickly immobilise either or both engines. All I need on the day is the safe combination from the store manager.'

Moody absorbed this information quietly, still slurping from his mug. He stretched it out a while longer before giving a single nod. 'You better not bugger this up, Bliss,' he said. 'Normally there's no way I'd let someone as raw as you anywhere near an undercover operation, but our esteemed Chief Inspector seems to think you're the ideal fit for the job. I wish I shared his confidence in you.'

'That makes two of us.'

Moody set his mug down on the desk and leaned forward. 'That'll be enough out of you, Detective Constable. I don't give a rat's arse if the DCI is bumming you on a regular basis and twice on Sundays. You keep on giving me verbals and you'll be off this job.'

'Ease up,' Bliss said before he could stop himself. 'I'm trying to lighten the atmosphere around here.'

'This isn't fucking Butlins, Constable. You don't get to wear a red jacket and laugh and joke about all day. This is a serious business, and undercover work is the most serious of them all. You stuff this up and it's us who have to pick up the pieces of you left behind by the O'Shea brothers.'

'Why do you automatically assume I'm going to fuck it up? I get that you don't like me. I get that you think I've been rushed through ahead of myself because of some influence from my old man. To be honest with you, Guv, I don't care about the first part of that. I'm never going to win a personality competition, and I can handle not being liked. But I'm telling you once and for all that my old man had nothing to do with how my career has gone. I've worked bloody hard for this, and I deserve it.'

With a loud snort by way of a riposte, Moody scowled at Bliss and said, 'And there in a nutshell is proof of why you don't.'

'Yeah, and how's that?'

'Because a decent detective would by now have worked out for himself how influential his father had been, albeit in the background, behind closed doors, with a few funny handshakes in drinking clubs with the brass.'

Bliss opened his mouth to respond, but snapped it shut again. He wanted to continue arguing, but in truth he was not as certain as Moody appeared to be. For the first time he questioned himself and his recent transition to detective. He had worked hard in uniform, studying every night and passing his exams with flying colours. He had earned the right to hang his uniform in the wardrobe and put his boots away in the cupboard. None of it had been handed to him on a plate. Yet Moody's words stung. Had his father whispered in the right ears to ease Jimmy's passage? Had money changed hands in brown envelopes? Had Dennis Bliss sold his soul to the brass in order to make life easier on his son?

'You have no reason to remove me from this case,' he said, pulling himself together. 'I have everything in hand. I've jumped through every hoop. I have the trust of these men, and a replacement at this late stage isn't going to work. You leave me in or you forget grabbing them up for the raid.'

The DI regarded him with scorn. 'It's a sad state we've come to when we have to rely on wet behind the ears children fresh out of uniform to do a real man's job.'

Moody was baiting him. Wanting him to push too hard and too far. But it wasn't going to work. Bliss needed this. And while it was true that an under-cover job on this scale had come early for him, he was convinced it wasn't too soon. He had John, Paul and

Ringo right where he wanted them, and after the job he was going to drive all three right into the hands of his CID colleagues. And after something O'Shea had let slip, there might be an even greater prize to be had.

'You'll see,' he said. It took some effort to swallow down his anger, but with the likes of Moody a show of temper now would serve to scupper everything he'd worked towards so far. 'I'll reel three hardened villains in and drop them in your net. Bagging them goes on your record as well as mine.'

The DI rose quickly from his seat. 'Yeah, so does any balls-up. You let that happen and me and you are finished.'

'And again, Guv, I'd like to thank you for that vote of confidence.'

The two men stood glaring at each other for a long moment, before Moody dismissed him. Bliss left the office without a further word. Seconds later, he popped his head around the door. 'I forgot to say, but you owe me a tenner. Saturday's result.'

Jimmy ducked back out of the office as Moody's rant began, and was at his desk a good thirty seconds before it subsided. DS Bradley met his eyes from his own desk directly opposite. 'Sucking up to the big man again, Jimmy?' he said, a wry grin twisting his lips.

'You know me, Sarge. I like to curry favour wherever I go.'

Bradley leaned back in his chair, crossing his legs. 'I've noticed that about you. Made a big impression on the rest of us.' He chortled and shook his head. 'I don't know what the Guv has against you, but rather you than me.'

Bliss wrinkled his nose. 'Ah, he'll be fine once he winds his neck in. You'll see. Soon as I have the other three Beatles banged up in the holding cells downstairs.'

'Yeah. That is if you don't fuck it up.'

'What is it with you people? Have a bit of faith, will you?' Bliss snapped back.

'That comes with time and experience, mate. I will have a fiver on it with you, though.'

'What, you're betting on me failing?'

Bradley laughed. 'Bloody right I am. Have to win back what you took off me over the weekend.'

Bliss sat there fuming, biting into his lower lip. At which point a deluge of plastic cups filled with rubber bands and paper clips came his way, the contents scattered all over him from head to toe like confetti. 'You bastards!' he roared, shooting to his feet and brushing away the debris. 'You bloody well had me going there.'

'You're too easy, Jimmy,' DC Faith Mitchell said as she walked by his desk, offering him her usual warm smile. 'Way, way too easy.'

Bliss grinned. Screw Moody. These men and women were the heart and soul of the team, and they had his back.

FIVE

ATER THAT AFTERNOON, WHILE Bliss's thoughts were on the sting operation he was due to be involved in, DC Mitchell looked his way after taking a phone call. 'I've got a job on,' she said. 'You want in?'

'Of course.'

'You didn't ask what it was.'

'No need. A job's a job.'

She flashed her straight white teeth. 'You'll learn.'

He liked Mitchell. She took zero amount of shit from anybody, and when called into action she could be a vicious, street-wise fighter. Many a mindless thug had underestimated her slight frame and pleasing looks. Off duty she wore her wavy dark brown hair down and long, but on duty it was always up in either a ponytail or braided in some way. Her features were already appealing, but when she broke out into that smile it took a lot to look away.

After running it by Moody, the pair hitched a ride in a patrol car to Victoria Park. During the short journey, Mitchell reeled off what she knew. A young mother had taken her toddler to play by the lake on the western fringe of the park. The boy had thrown a strop when she decided to take a break for a cup of tea, so she'd left him standing outside the pavilion café while she fetched them both a drink and a snack. Her eyes were on him the whole time other than when she collected her change, but when she came back out, the boy was gone and nobody had seen what became of him.

Bliss closed his eyes and muttered beneath his breath. Mitchell cottoned on immediately to his train of thinking. 'Our people at the scene are pretty sure the boy didn't go into the lake. Apparently, there were a lot of kids and parents right by the edge. Their attention was on the lake, which is why nobody noticed what was going on behind them near the café. But the word is there's no way he fell in and drowned.'

'Let's hope he's just wandered off, then,' Bliss said. 'I don't want to think about the alternatives.'

'First uniforms on scene called for a lot of backup to help search the park. We were asked to attend in case this is more than a lost kid.'

The promising early morning had become a bright and sunny May day. A breeze took the edge off the heat, but Bliss felt it prickle his flesh all the same when they stepped out of the vehicle.

Victoria Park was the first public open space to be developed specifically for the people. The parkland opened its doors in the mid-1800s, its development continuing for decades afterwards, taking up over two hundred acres of what had previously been poor quality land used for gravel digging, market gardens and grazing. Bliss knew just about every inch of it, having played in its fields and by its lakes countless times as a kid. When he and Mitchell arrived on scene, the lake and pavilion had been sealed off with tape. A number of officers stood guard, preventing the public from entering the cordon. The café had been cleared of all but essential emergency workers, and it was in there that they found Sergeant Moore, the duty officer, directing operations.

He was the kind of copper who made civilians feel secure. Most people would have to look up to him, and when they did they'd notice his keen eyes and the firm set of his jaw.

'We have Mrs Lawson tucked away in the back office,' he told them. 'There's a WPC in with her. No sign of the boy as yet.'

'You're interviewing all members of the public who were here by the lake at the time the boy went missing?' Mitchell asked him.

'Yep. We have them corralled in the playground area and they are making statements as we speak. I've arranged for Hendon to bus in trainees to help with the search, and I already have as many bodies as could be spared out there running grid patterns.'

'Brilliant. You seem to have everything in hand. We'll have a word with the mother. Stupid question, I realise, but how is she coping?'

Moore winced as if what he was about to say pained him. 'In deep shock, I think. She keeps referring to the boy as if he's a different age. She initially told us he was a toddler, so we're thinking perhaps two or three. She mentioned a buggy, and there is one left outside after everybody else claimed theirs. But she also said a couple of things that don't quite chime, giving me the impression of an older kid.'

'What's the boy's name?' Bliss asked.

'Michael.'

'And Mrs Lawson's first name?'

'Angie.'

Bliss nodded. 'Thanks. We'll send your WPC out while we speak to the mother. Is it okay by you if she stands by to step back into the room if we need her to?'

Sergeant Moore agreed. Bliss and Faith Mitchell made themselves comfortable in the office and introduced themselves to Angie Lawson. The first thing she did was ask if they had any news, and their response prompted a fresh welling of tears. She mopped her nose with a balled-up tissue, eyes raw from weeping, her neck and cheeks flushed. Her hair was limp and straggly, and to Bliss it looked as if she wore no makeup. The woman also seemed undernourished, and he wondered if there was more to her hand tremor than adrenaline flooding her veins.

'Can we get you anything, Angie?' Bliss asked. 'A cup of tea, perhaps? Glass of water?'

She looked at him for a moment as if she didn't quite understand what he was asking. Then the penny seemed to drop and she cleared her throat. 'They... they gave me some orange squash. All I want is my son back.'

'Of course. We're doing everything we can. I know you've already spoken to a couple of our uniformed colleagues, but we'd like a quick chat if you're up to it.'

Angie Lawson stiffened, the hand holding a tissue pausing halfway towards her eyes. She blinked at him. 'Will it help find my boy?'

'It might.'

She nodded slowly and sat back in her chair. After waiting a few seconds for the traumatised woman to gather herself, DC Mitchell got straight down to business. 'Has anybody contacted your husband, Angie?'

Lawson frowned, then shook her head. 'No. He's... he's abroad. He travels a lot, and I didn't want to worry him until I knew there was something to worry him about.'

'That sounds sensible. At this stage we're operating on the understanding that your son wandered off, and would hope our extensive search will locate him quickly for you.'

'Yes. Thank you. That's what the sergeant told me.'

'Michael is how old?' Bliss asked. He knew he ought to have let his colleague take the lead. They were the same rank, but she had several years on him when it came to experience. He kept his focus on the distraught mother rather than catch sight of his colleague's disapproving glance.

The response was not immediate, however. Bliss saw the woman retreat inside herself. He glanced at Mitchell and frowned. She shrugged and nodded at him to push on. 'Angie?' he prompted.

'He'll be six next birthday.' The pitch of her voice rose as she spoke, sounding more like a question than a statement.

'Is that right? Only, Sergeant Moore seems to think you told him your son was a toddler.'

She gave a harsh, dry laugh. 'I think of him that way is all. Mikey is still my little boy.'

'And yet you left a buggy outside the café. A five-year-old wouldn't need a buggy.'

After a moment of apparent confusion, Lawson shook her head. 'No, no. You don't understand. Mikey has bad hips. He sometimes needs the buggy by the time we head home from here.'

Bliss nodded. 'I see. Well, that explains that little mystery.'

'You come here a lot?' Mitchell asked.

'Two or three times a week.'

Bliss gave that some thought. If she was a regular, the pair might have been spotted and stalked, some nonce perhaps observing potential easy prey. The thought turned his stomach. There was something else bothering him, too. He didn't like to make assumptions, but to look at Mrs Lawson he would never have imagined her with a young son. She had to be on the wrong side of forty, and though that didn't rule her out it made him feel uneasy about her story.

'What's Michael's date of birth?' he asked.

'Oh, that's easy. He was my Valentine's Day gift. Fourteenth of February.'

'How lovely. What year?'

Angie Lawson arched her eyebrows as if puzzled by the question. 'I told you, he's five. He was born in sixty-four.' She smiled as her mind took her elsewhere once more. 'Friday's child is loving and giving. Just like my Mikey.'

SIX

STANDARD OPERATING PROCEDURE WITHIN the Beatles gang dictated that Bliss called the number of a public phone box at the same time every evening. He rotated between four boxes when placing the calls, making a random decision as to which one he would use. He felt his senses tingling every time he approached one of them, and on this Monday evening it was no different.

He was his usually vigilant self when looking for a shadow that shouldn't be there. As he made his way along the street, Bliss concentrated on people who kept their heads down. He also made a point of checking the interiors of parked cars to see if there was anybody sitting in one acting as if they were minding their own business. He noticed nothing out of the ordinary. In this location, two phone boxes stood back to back. On a whim, he chose the one on the left.

Jimmy was early, but he waited out the time inside. He wished John had given them all mobile phones. There were plenty falling off the backs of lorries these days that would set you back no more than a monkey, and a couple of grand for four of them wouldn't have broken the bank. As the seconds ticked away, he stepped back out and ducked into the other box. He couldn't put his finger on why. His undercover operation was fully sanctioned and monitored at every stage, so if for some reason either or both of the phones were currently being traced as part of a different case, he knew he'd be able to talk his way out of trouble. He had learned to be wary, nonetheless. He had no idea if the gang suspected him, but if they did, then Paul or Ringo could easily be out there observing the boxes while he made the call to John. It didn't hurt to put on an appropriate act.

He dialled. It rang out four times before his call was answered.

'It's George,' he said. They were the only two words he ever spoke during these phone conversations. The rest of the time he listened.

'We're in play,' John told him. The man's voice carried not a single trace of emotion. Bliss felt his own breath catch in his chest and lodge there for a moment. This was what he had been waiting for these past three weeks. 'Friday. You have work to do, Georgie boy. Get it done, and don't fuck up.'

Was there anyone who trusted him to see this through?

That was it. Moving back out into the cool evening air, Bliss took several deep breaths. In his blues he had been involved in dozens of arrests, and had operated as part of the backup team on twice as many more. But this was easily the biggest investigation of his career so far. And so soon after he had made detective. Less than two months into the job and here he was working undercover on a planned heist. This was major league, and he couldn't afford to blow it.

No stress there, then.

Hazel was out for the night with friends, so Bliss dropped into one of his locals for a swift pint before heading home. This was one of the neighbourhood's 50-50 pubs – fifty percent villains and fifty percent coppers. There were two unspoken rules, but they made the combination work. First, the coppers didn't talk shop with their opposite numbers. No vying for inside information on scores being planned. Second, no hardcore faces. Having armed blaggers and the like drinking alongside the men and women who were after them made the atmosphere tense, and that was bad for business.

Such boozers were where coppers brought their blind eyes, and villains left their loose tongues tied up outside before entering. The two opposing groups tolerated each other, and drawn lines became muddy. A

50-50 was the kind of place a man who made a living out of selling hooky VHS films could safely go to sell their wares, and were just as likely to have coppers as they were faces for customers. Such a relationship was strictly forbidden and completely illegal, of course, but it went on right across the country.

When Bliss had asked his father how these mixed pubs were considered acceptable, the old man had told him that stains you picked up by trading with these small time villains were easily washed off when you took into account the volume of information leakage despite the informal agreements. Street informants and nudge-nudge relationships were created in these pubs, and his father had always accrued far more than he ever gave away in return.

The Bliss family's true local was a way station for criminal intelligence, and everybody involved looked the other way and asked no contentious questions. This boozer was not in the same league, and here Bliss was virtually unknown by either group. A decent place to sit and relax over a beer.

During the thirty minutes he sat alone with his drink, Bliss was offered duty-free cigarettes and booze, pirated films, a line in raw-silk shirts, Adidas trainers, and a shot at a time share in Marbella. He waved them away with good grace, and nobody took offence.

For a short while he stared into the distance, his thoughts having turned to Angie Lawson and her missing son. If the boy was indeed missing. If he had ever existed at all. Her confused state was enough for DC Mitchell to call a halt to their questioning, immediately summoning a doctor to check her out. Because this prolonged the initial stage of the investigation, Bliss ran out of time and had to cadge a lift back to the station. He'd wished Faith well and made himself scarce, but he couldn't help wondering what was going on inside Angie Lawson's head.

As he finished his drink, a woman slid into the chair opposite and almost dropped her highball tumbler on the scarred wooden table. Her drink slopped out, making an island out of her glass. She giggled, belched and giggled some more. Heavy makeup made her face look ghost-like, but her wide blue eyes and perfect ruby-red mouth drew lustful gazes from men of all ages.

'How's tricks, Elaine?' he asked.

She cackled, pointing an unsteady finger at him. 'You always say that. Like I don't know what you mean. But I do, Jimmy Bliss. I do.'

Elaine was a street prostitute. Bliss had lost count of the number of times he'd tried to persuade her to become an in-house escort instead. It wasn't a great living, but it was a good deal safer than working the streets. On numerous occasions she had shown up to meetings with severe bruising, the odd laceration, and even a broken nose. From what he could tell, Elaine took it all in her stride. She knew she'd be safe with Bliss, though, especially since she was also one of his valued confidential informants.

With a dramatic flourish, Elaine tossed her hair and crossed one leg over the other, revealing her stocking tops. Bliss knew she was probably wearing little or no underwear, and currently offering some keen observer a teasing glimpse. From where he sat he could see little, and was glad of it. He liked Elaine, but there were some reactions men were simply unable to control, and he did not want her getting the wrong impression of him.

'You have anything for me?' he asked. 'Or is this purely a coincidence?'

'Nah. I just happened to fancy a drink and this was the closest boozer, is all.'

'You're done for the night, then?'

'Probably. Unless you're up for a quickie round the back.'

'I don't think so. But thanks for the kind offer. Sweetheart, I can see you're more than a bit tipsy, and as I'm about to leave I think I should walk you home.'

She tilted her head to one side as if examining him closely. He noticed something pass across her eyes: a curious mix of self-doubt and gratitude. She leaned across the table. 'You sure you want to be seen with the likes of me outside of this drum?'

Bliss frowned. 'What's wrong with the likes of you? You're a nicer, smarter woman than many I've come across. You shouldn't think less of yourself because of what you do for a living, Elaine.'

'Don't,' she said, sweeping up her glass and draining its contents.

'Don't what?'

'Don't pity me.'

'I'm not. I wouldn't.'

'Then don't be kind to me, either.'

Bliss sat back and waited for her to look up for his response. 'Somebody should be. Including you. What you do is what you do, Elaine. It's not who you are. You're pretty, you're funny, you're bright. Don't ever sell yourself short.'

Elaine snorted. 'Aw, Jimmy. Are you Richard Gere to my Julia Roberts?'

He had seen the film *Pretty Woman*, so he knew what she was referring to. He smiled and shook his head. 'I'm no rich man trying to cross some divide here, Elaine. But look, you don't embarrass me. I am not embarrassed to be seen with you, in or out of this place. To be blunt with you, you're not Elaine the brass to me. You're Elaine the person.'

'You just don't… fancy me, is that right?'

'Why d'you say that?'

'Because in all the time I've known you, you've never taken me up on my offer of a freebie.'

'It's not like that at all. I'm seeing someone.'

Elaine snorted. 'Most of the men I give a hand job to are seeing someone, Jimmy. They're still perfectly happy to shell out for a tug from me instead. That or the blowie their wives begrudgingly give them only on their anniversary.'

'Not my style, sweetheart. I'll happily sit here and have a chat with you, I'll even walk you home and make sure you get there safely, but that's as far as it can go. Not because I don't like you, just because I'm with somebody else and that means something to me. Okay?'

Bliss liked to have his back to the wall, looking out on any room in which he sat. It was something his father had suggested he do, so that nobody could sneak up on him. He'd secured a table that allowed him to face both the bar and the door, which opened as he happened to be looking directly at it.

He froze.

Bliss made a rapid calculation. There was no way for him to make a dash for the toilet or hide himself away in another part of the pub without being noticed by the newcomer. He thought quickly and reached a snap decision.

'Elaine,' he said, in a low voice only she could hear. 'I hope you're not too sozzled to understand me. Whatever happens in the next few minutes, go along with me, right?'

'What?'

'Some geezer who just came in might stop by the table. I don't want him to know who I am, okay. Police business. If it comes up, I'm Vincent. Vincent Styles. You and me know each other, but we're acquaintances at best. Got it?'

'Jimmy, what the fuck are you on about?'

'Just tell me you understand!'

His gaze tore into hers, eyes pleading for her to roll with it. Because, as he'd expected from the moment he saw who had entered the pub, he'd been spotted. And now Declan O'Shea was making his way between the tables towards them.

'Well, well, well,' O'Shea said, a wide grin plastering itself across his face. 'Fancy running into you. You all right there, Vincent?'

Bliss nodded, trying to imagine how his character might react to the chance encounter. If that's what it was. 'Yeah, I'm all right. You?'

'Always.' His eyes darted across to Elaine, and the first lines of a frown appeared on his face.

Bliss decided not to introduce Elaine to him. The less he involved her the better. 'Fancy a drink?' he asked.

The big man glanced around the pub. 'No, you're all right. I'm meeting somebody.'

'Next time, maybe.'

'Yeah. Have to say, I'm surprised to run into you around these parts, Vincent.'

About to reply, Bliss was left open mouthed when Elaine turned her head, looked up at the newcomer and said, 'Vinnie and me go back. He pops over to see me once a month or so.'

Before O'Shea could jump back in with a question, Bliss said, 'Yeah, we hung around together back in the day. Lived on the same floor of a tower block in Walthamstow. Eighteen floors up in the sky you get to know your neighbours really well.'

O'Shea was nodding, looking between the two of them. 'I can well believe it. I know a few of those sky-scrapers. Which one was yours?'

Bliss swallowed. They had already reached the domino effect of telling lies. You knocked one down, others were certain to follow. He'd made a mistake in mentioning a tower block. He could think of an estate containing three of them built close together, but had no idea what any of them were named.

'Walter Savill,' Elaine said. 'Nice enough when they were first put up, I suppose. Bit of a shit-hole when we both lived there, though.'

Bliss felt a narrow band of tension squeeze behind his eyes. Declan O'Shea was hard to read, but he didn't think the big Irishman had bought the story. He might not know exactly what was going on, but he knew something was amiss. That much was clear in the way he regarded the pair of them at the table.

'You sure about that drink?' Bliss said, hoping the bluff didn't work against him. The longer he remained sitting there, the greater chance of somebody else he knew stopping by for a chat. Somebody who might use his real name.

For a time that felt too long, O'Shea made no reply. But eventually he nodded and started to turn away. 'Another time, Vincent. I have a bit of business to attend to. I'll be seeing you, though.'

What did that mean?

Blowing out the breath he'd been holding, Bliss kept his tongue until O'Shea was on the other side of the stairway and sidling up to the bar. 'Drink up,' he said to Elaine, picking up his own glass. 'Let's get out of here before he changes his mind.'

Elaine knew better than to ask questions. She had played along, and that was what counted. He thanked her for helping him out and laughed off the encounter as if it were of little importance. After making sure she got home safely, he took off in the direction of his parents' house with ruby-red lip marks on his cheek.

He smiled at the thought, but the closer he came to reaching his own home the more the smile faded from his lips.

His undercover package included a flat in Leyton, a mile from the tower blocks he'd mentioned. His being in Bethnal Green for a drink was no big deal, but Declan O'Shea would be wondering why on this particular night when he himself was drinking there. Two men who supposedly lived nowhere close to the area, happening to be in the same boozer at the same time, was something the big man was bound to find suspicious. Bliss's reaction to the tower block question would hardly have put the other man at ease.

It was a concern, but given more thinking time he knew he'd be able to explain it away. He was thankful that Elaine had had the presence of mind to say the right thing at the right time, especially in her condition. He bit into his bottom lip and turned his thoughts to other concerns.

As he rubbed away Elaine's lipstick, his mind turned to Hazel. Moving out of the only home he had ever known was a big deal, leaving the area bigger still. These streets had become his sanctuary over the years. All of his memories were here, trapped within old soot-stained walls and new breeze blocks alike. The knowledge that one day soon he would no longer follow this path home after grabbing a quick pint began to disturb him. His stomach churned at the thought.

Bliss had never had any qualms about being a home boy. Unlike many lads his age who could not wait to flee the nest as soon as they left school – some joining the forces, others choosing to make their own way in the world elsewhere – he loved living at home. He had two great parents, both of whom would do anything for him. His mother coddled him, and while his dad could be strict, he understood it was for his own good. To raise a decent family you needed discipline, and he was taught values from an early age.

It was, perhaps, one of the reasons why he didn't frown upon the likes of Elaine. Or, more to the point, what she did for a living. Some people saw selling your body for sex as horrific and amoral. The way he looked at it, she was utilising her physical assets in the best way she knew how. Over the course of several drinks, he'd begun to know the young woman quite well. Her parents had constantly sniped at her when she was younger, telling anyone who cared to listen that their daughter would never amount to anything because she was too thick and too ugly.

Bliss had seen that for what it was: parents unable to contend with her intellect, and feeling ashamed of having a child who was manifestly brighter than they were. As a result, they put her down, stamping upon her free will and right to self-expression. They left their daughter feeling out of place and unworthy. Their treatment of Elaine became a self-fulfilling prophecy, as she turned to wantonness as a way of getting noticed, of attracting attention. She moved easily from flirtation to sex, and slipping into prostitution when money was tight had been a natural progression.

Living nearby, Bliss had observed this from a distance. His own interactions with Elaine were on a different plane, and he saw beyond the tacky clothes and dubious language. She was actually one of the local characters he would miss most of all when he and Hazel moved in together, though telling his parents that might raise the odd quizzical glance in his direction. They were easy-going people, but they clearly wanted greater things for their son than for him to befriend a hooker.

Now that he thought about it, he didn't imagine Hazel taking kindly to it, either.

SEVEN

THE SPECIAL OPERATIONS TEAM met the following morning after briefing. Nominally, DI Moody was in charge of the day-to-day management, but on this occasion, DCI England chaired the meeting, and appeared keen to tick all remaining boxes.

'I understand you got the nod last night,' he said to Bliss. 'Friday night is a go.'

Bliss paused to take a breath. He was nervous, especially given what he was about to do. 'Yes, sir.'

'So the gang are fully prepared. Are we?'

'We are, sir. At least, as far as our original plan is concerned.'

To his right, Moody's head jerked up as if somebody had touched a cattle prod against his genitals. England peered at Bliss over his reading glasses. 'And what exactly does that mean?' he asked stiffly.

Something had been niggling at Bliss since he and his fellow Beatles had met in the snooker hall. At first he was unable to pinpoint it, but the snippet of conversation that had become stuck in his subconscious eventually worked its way loose. In the early hours of the morning he'd got up, gone downstairs to the kitchen to make himself a hot chocolate, and at the dining table formulated a new plan.

'It means I would like to suggest a different strategy, sir. I'm sorry, but I haven't had time to run this by DI Moody, as it only came to me while we were all entering the room.' In truth, he hadn't spoken to his DI about it because he was certain that Moody would either hate the idea and dismiss it out of hand, or like it and claim it as his own. The man would never forgive him for this, but the two worked together about as well as Simon and Garfunkel, so there was no relationship to ruin.

'It's a bit late in the game to discuss a new approach, Bliss,' Moody snapped. 'Why don't you do yourself a favour and let it go?'

Bliss would never know if that's what he would have done had nobody intervened, but DCI England did. He wanted to know more, and demanded Bliss explain himself.

'Sir, during the meeting I had with the gang last Thursday, a remark was made which I initially missed.

It must have stuck with me, though, because I just realised what it meant. What it *could* mean.'

'Okay. Spit it out, man.'

'John – that is Declan O'Shea – slipped up, I think, when he mentioned his brother, Dermot. He reeled off a list of silent contributions his brother had made to the planning of the heist, but finished off with something peculiar. He said his brother also had the connection to the man in charge.'

This sent a ripple of chatter spreading out across the room. England held up a hand, glanced at DI Moody and focussed on Bliss once more. 'Are you sure that's what you heard, Constable?'

'Absolutely. It didn't make any real impression until I remembered it. But, if that is the case, if there is somebody else above the O'Shea brothers, then I think that changes everything.'

'I would have to agree. In what way do you see things now panning out?'

Bliss was grateful that the DCI was taking charge. Moody would have shut it all down by now, demanding to find out more from Bliss in the sanctity of his office. This way, Jimmy managed to outline his entire plan in front of the team as a whole.

'Sir, the original plan was always about taking down the O'Shea brothers. Scooping up the other two Beatles was a nice enough coup, but with what I have on tape and in eventually catching Declan with his hands on the stolen cash, we always believed we'd have enough to wrap both brothers up in a neat package. Only now, if there is another rung on the ladder above those two, we must be talking about a heavy-duty villain.'

'Such as?'

'Could be any of them. But the most likely to be into armed blags and have links to the O'Shea brothers are the Smiths or Tyrone Griffin. Whoever it is, I think it's worth going after them as well.'

'You mean breaking Declan and Dermot O'Shea in the interview room?' Moody sneered. He scoffed and shook his head. 'Not a chance. Don't be so bloody naïve, Bliss. They might have no answer to your undercover tapes and us catching them with their hands in the sweet jar, but the moment you ask them about anyone higher up the food chain they'll effectively spread superglue on their lips.'

'I agree,' Bliss said. 'That's why I'm not planning to do it that way.'

'So what are you suggesting we do?'

'I think we leave the arrests until later. The way I see it, if there's a man in charge he must be getting his cut. One of the O'Sheas, if not both of them, is going to hand that off sooner rather than later. Declan's plan was always for us to split off into two motors and meet up the following day at the snooker hall to divvy up our shares, but ours was to immobilise one getaway vehicle and have all four Beatles in the one motor when you take us down. I say we do the same thing, but we let O'Shea drive us off. If he goes straight to his brother's contact we can take them there and then. If there's a delay, if he happens to drop the three of us off first, we watch and wait. I think the big fish is worth the risk.'

'The risk of blowing the entire operation?' Moody bellowed, getting to his feet as if to emphasise his apparent outrage at the suggestion. 'Your great plan is to ignore the sitting ducks we have trapped inside the vehicle with the money, and instead to let O'Shea go on the off chance that he might lead us to some Mr Big we're only hearing about for the first time here and now?'

'If we do it properly, Guv, we stand to gain so much more. But, in fact we risk very little. I'm not saying we allow them to go their separate ways. My instinct tells me O'Shea always intended to take this Mr Big's cut to him immediately, and my bet is he still will even if we're all with him. If he doesn't, you can still take us down if you decide that's the way to go, or you can let him drop us off and track him to wherever he goes next.'

'And what makes you think he's going to drive you all anywhere? He could simply bugger off with the entire haul.'

Bliss shook his head. 'No. If he'd not given us his name, or given a false one, I'd say you were right. But he coughed to being Declan O'Shea, so he's bringing us our cut. If we pull this off, he's going to want to use us again. He does that by keeping us sweet, not having us after his guts because he's mugged us off. But, if you're anxious about that aspect, I can always make sure the only working car is the one I'm behind the wheel of. He can hardly turf me out without raising eyebrows.'

'This requires a lot more boots on the ground,' England said, a phrase he had doubtlessly brought with him from his time in the army. 'We're going to need additional surveillance. Having an either-or end game requires us to have teams available for both possibilities.'

Bliss nodded, starting to relax into the new game plan. 'I understand the difficulties, sir. I also realise there will be extra costs involved. I just think we have an opportunity to net someone larger than the pool we were originally fishing in. We'll still have Declan and Dermot O'Shea, that I can confidently promise you. And we can still settle for that if you prefer. I'm of the opinion that when a chance like this presents itself, you should try to take it.'

'One of the benefits of being a lower rank, DC Bliss. If I go with your plan, it's not you who gets his Jacobs cut off by the powers that be. It's me.'

'With respect, sir, I won't emerge unscathed. Such a balls-up will follow me around like a bad smell for the rest of my career.'

TONY J FORDER

England regarded him with renewed interest. 'You may have a point. And yet you're willing to kill that career before it's truly begun?'

'No, sir. I'm not. I don't regard it as a risk, not really. Provided we plan with care and precision, we'll end up with exactly what we'd originally hoped for at the very least, and perhaps a great deal more. That's a win-win in my book.'

Seconds later, the DCI relented and allowed the group to discuss the matter openly. Many experienced detectives sat on the fence and were happy to talk in vague terms rather than offer anything meaningful that might be used against them if the operation fell flat on its face. Others were far more enthusiastic. As Bliss took them all through it one more time, expanding on the specifics, he could see England nodding more frequently and relaxing back into his chair. That was when he knew he had the man.

As for Moody, his name had always matched his attitude, and he made it clear at every juncture that he remained firmly against revising the plan they had all been working on for more than three weeks. Bliss understood the man's position. He had devised the original strategy, and he certainly did not want Bliss getting any credit for taking it one stage further and adding a significantly bigger name to their catch. Equally, it couldn't harm him if he set himself against making changes. There would be a price to pay eventually for not running the idea by Moody first, but Bliss was content. He had done the right thing. And as his father had told him, a man could always live with his decisions provided he did that.

EIGHT

'WHAT THE FUCK WAS that?' Moody snapped.

He had summoned Bliss into his office. The two men stood toe-to-toe, and the DI was snarling into Bliss's face.

'What was what, Guv?' Bliss kept his gaze even and his tone flat.

'That steaming pile of dog shit we waded through back there. Are you really going to stand there and insist you came up with that plan on the spur of the moment first thing this morning?'

Bliss's father had given him many pieces of advice. One of them came to mind, and he couldn't let go of it. There would come a time when he would have to decide what kind of copper he wanted to be. One who took the easy route, stayed beneath the radar, and didn't rock the boat, or one who put the job above personal ambitions. Jimmy had not expected to have to make that decision this early, but if he took a backward step now he was showing Moody what kind of copper he intended to be. This moment would forever be etched upon the DI's mind. Instead, Bliss stood firm.

'No, I'm not,' he said. 'But, if you really want to know why I said that, it's because I don't trust you.'

'You don't… What do you think this is, Bliss? A bloody nursery? You don't get to trust or not trust me. You get to do what you're told whether you like it or not. I'm your bloody superior!'

'In rank, maybe. In point of fact, you're my senior officer, not my superior.'

Moody stuck his face in closer. 'Yeah, and rank is all that bloody matters, you insolent little tripehound. You want a piece of me, Bliss, you and I can take a walk around to the back of the building and go at it. But until that happens, you do as I fucking tell you to do. Is that clear?'

Bliss licked his lips. 'Yes, Guv. It is.'

'Good. I thought you might see sense once I explained the facts of life to you.'

'Yes, Guv. You want us to leave our jackets in here?'

'Leave our… what are you on about, man?'

'I assumed you'd want to remove your jacket before you rolled up your sleeves. I know I do.'

This time Moody blew out his breath in a steady stream, his neck and cheeks burning red. 'Oh, I get it. You think because you did a bit of boxing when you were younger you can take me, right? Well, here's a lesson for you, Bliss: don't ever assume. I won't be using no Queensbury rules if you and me go at it. I fight dirty, and I fight to win. You and me end up going a round, I'll batter you.'

Bliss eyed him up and down. Moody had the height and the build, he was in decent shape, and he had all the hallmarks of a scrapper; from the bent nose to the scarred, bony knuckles. 'You might do,' he admitted. 'But the one thing you'll know when we're done, *Guvnor*, is that you've been in a fight. And over what? Getting all bent out of shape because I showed you up? Well, you're bloody right I did. And that's nobody's fault but your own. If I could trust you, I would have come to you first. As it turns out, you've treated me like shit since I arrived here, so if you want to do this, let's go and get it over with. If that ends up with me transferred out or fired, I don't give a shit. But if you threaten me, be prepared for me to react. You want to slap me around, well get ready to be on the end of a few clumps of your own.'

Perhaps it was the way he said it: a calm, steady voice betraying not an ounce of the anxiety he truly felt. Or maybe it was simply a case of Moody realising how unprofessionally he was behaving at that specific moment. Either way, the DI regarded him for a full ten seconds before turning away and walking behind his desk. He removed his jacket, draped it over the back of his chair, then took his seat.

'Do you know why you were chosen for this job, Bliss?' he eventually asked. The colour in his face had leached away along with his anger. He continued before Jimmy had a chance to respond. 'This undercover operation has been in the making for months, not the weeks you've been a DC. The proper, experienced detective due to have played your role, is off work following a ruck with a couple of burglars. And don't assume you were the next choice, either. The problem with the next bloke was his thick Geordie accent. No, the reason you strolled into this job for which you are entirely unsuited, Detective *Constable* Bliss, is that you are similar in build and looks to the man who was supposed to play the role of Vincent Styles. And you happen to speak with the same accent.'

Bliss had wondered why he was chosen, but had never asked. He didn't care. To him, it was part of the job, and he felt confident about taking it on. He wasn't naïve enough not to take into consideration his lack of experience, but he hadn't walked into CID straight out of Hendon training college. Eight years in uniform had honed his skillset and his ability to work under all kinds of pressure.

'If you think that rattles me or embarrasses me, think again,' he said. 'I don't care if my name came up after the cleaner's. I'm not stupid. I knew this had to have been a long-term plan, and that I must be filling in for somebody else. But so what? It's either me or cancel the job, and there's been too much investment to do that.'

'You think you can pull this off, Bliss?'

'Guv, my reputation – well, the legend attached to Vince Styles, anyway – was built to withstand close scrutiny. Thankfully, whatever happened to the previous Vincent Styles did so before he and the other Beatles met for the first time. If I physically match the general description of this safecracker extraordinaire, and that made me a good fit, so be it. So far I've managed to fool my fellow Beatles into believing I am him, and also that I can do the job. If I can't persuade you of the same thing ahead of time, then I suppose it's going to have to be the result that counts.'

'Yet you've just gone and made the job a lot bloody harder.'

Bliss sighed. 'Aren't you even mildly curious? Don't you want to know who this man is? The kind of man hardened villains like the O'Shea brothers defer to. You went into this to get them, because it was thought they were at the top of the food chain. Now we know different. I, for one, won't be satisfied if we end up landing the same catch. And we will still reel them in. I guarantee it.'

Moody hooked into that. 'You stake your own reputation on it, do you, Bliss?'

'I think I already am.'

'And how about your career?'

'Same thing at the end of the day. If whatever goodwill I've built up in this job so far gets flushed down the pan after this operation, my career goes with it. I'll never be more than a DC, and I may not be that for much longer.'

'Then why take the risk?'

Bliss realised for the first time exactly who and what DI Moody was. He was the first type of copper his father had described. The kind Bliss had decided he did not want to be. He regarded his boss with all the contempt he could muster, and said, 'Because despite what you think of me, I *am* a real copper. I don't want any old result. I want the right one. And shame on you for not wanting the same.'

At his desk a short while later, Bliss noticed a few faces turned his way. Most were sympathetic, others respectful, while one or two revealed their allegiance to DI Moody by proffering scowls. He ignored them all and put his head down to catch up on paperwork. DC Mitchell walked by his desk and offered him a chocolate digestive; an open demonstration of her approval. He took the biscuit and made her a cup of tea as a way of showing his gratitude.

'Don't let moody Moody get beneath your skin,' she said, as they chatted by the table set aside for breaktime. 'He's a man who goes with the flow pretty much every time.'

'I see that now,' Bliss said. 'I just can't work out why he hates me to such a degree.'

'You already have.' She sniggered at his apparent bemusement. 'You said it yourself, Jimmy. He thinks your dad worked some magic to get you this job. He resents that because he had nobody on the inside to help him.'

'You're kidding, right? He actually thinks my old man put a word in?'

'Yeah. And you don't?'

Bliss opened his mouth to reply, but stopped short. Did he know that for sure? His father had said it wasn't the case, but had he lied to pacify his son and quell his curiosity?

'I didn't,' he said eventually. 'But now you have me wondering.'

Mitchell shrugged. 'So what if he did? Big deal. We all do what we can to make it. If you didn't ask for a leg-up, you can still hold your head high. My guess is, you made DC all on your own, and if your dad had any influence at all it was to get you placed in this nick.'

Bliss thought about that. He'd never had any doubts about his father's word beforehand. He didn't like doubting him now. But if what Faith had said was correct, if that was all the old man had done, he could live with it. And DI Moody would have to learn to deal with it, too.

A moment later, Mitchell was back by his side. 'You have a window in your busy schedule?' she asked.

He checked his wristwatch. 'I do. No more briefings as far as I'm aware.'

'Good. Let's go and do some proper police work.'

NINE

THE DÉCOR AND ATMOSPHERE within the psychiatric wing at the Mile End Hospital was a lot less grim than its exterior. The ward was situated in one of the oldest parts of the Victorian building, its soot-stained walls originally constructed as an infirmary for the local workhouse. Bright lights and pastel paintwork provided a visual tonic, but as he and DC Mitchell found their way to the head of department's office, Bliss decided he'd rather never visit it again. He realised mental ill-health wasn't contagious, but he did wonder if any of the doctors there might spot something inside him to concern themselves with.

Mr Yarwood, the chief consultant, met with the two detectives for ten minutes before accompanying them to the room in which Angie Lawson was being kept. As soon as the doctor had given his approval the previous afternoon, DC Mitchell had taken Lawson back to Bethnal Green station. When her questioning resumed, the woman continued to speak as if time were shifting while they sat in the interview room. She appeared to be firm on most things, but never wavered in her conviction that her missing son was five years old and had been born in the mid-sixties. The assistant chief constable had wasted no time in authorising Mitchell's recommendation for a section order.

His colleague had filled Bliss in on how deep she had been able to dig over the past day, the consultant filling in some missing pieces when they all gathered in his office. As they reached Lawson's room, Bliss felt the leaden weight of dread deep in the pit of his stomach. Nothing good was going to emerge from this next conversation. All they could do was contain the situation somehow.

The first thing Angie did when they entered her room was to ask if they had found Michael. Yarwood's earlier advice had been to pacify the woman as often as possible, and definitely not to add fuel to her obvious psychological distress. It had been agreed that a simple lie would help calm her fears, after which she might attempt to engage with them again. Both Bliss and Mitchell had argued for a wider framework, seeking permission to use her own words as a guide if they thought it might help them make progress. Yarwood had reluctantly agreed.

'Michael is fine,' Mitchell said. She offered a reassuring smile. 'We found him not far away from the pavilion. He wasn't afraid, and he's quite safe and physically unharmed. But the doctors are looking him over to be clinically certain.'

'When can I see him?'

Bliss thought her response was off. She was neither relieved nor agitated. It was as if her immediate reaction was designed to fit in with what they might have expected of her. The words were right, but they lacked genuine emotion.

'Soon enough,' he said. 'But your son is being taken care of, so you don't have to fret. Meanwhile, because of the disruption caused by him going missing, we do still need to ask you some questions.'

Lawson eased back in her chair and nodded. She said nothing.

DC Mitchell took it up from there. 'Angie, when you and Michael first went to the park from your home yesterday, you were pushing the buggy but he was walking by your side, is that right?'

Nodding this time, the woman said, 'Yes. Always to my right so he never went close to the traffic.' Her finger pointed to where he might be if he were standing by her side now.

'And he never had to use the buggy during that walk? Not even once?'

'No. He'd get tired after playing and running around, and his hips ached, so he'd only ever need pushing on the way home.'

'Do you always hold his hand when you walk together?'

'Of course.'

'How do you manage to steer the buggy with just the one hand?'

'I… don't know. I just manage. It makes my wrist ache a bit.'

'I can imagine. Tell me, Angie, between the time you arrived at the park and the time you first noticed Michael missing, did you bump your head on anything? Take a fall, perhaps? Stumble over something?'

Lawson seemed to consider the question, but then shook her head. 'No. Nothing like that. I'm sure I would've remembered. Even if I didn't, I'd have a bump or a cut or something, and I haven't.'

'Quite. So, let me ask you this, Angie: would it surprise you to know that we've been able to trace part of your journey to the park on our street surveillance system?'

This time the woman shrugged. 'Not really. Starting to see more and more of them cameras around. The ones on the poles.'

'That's true. But I'm guessing it *would* surprise you to learn that at no point during that journey was your son ever walking alongside you.'

Angie Lawson barked a quick, guttural laugh. She turned her gaze on Faith. 'What are you saying? You think my Mikey's a bloody ghost or something?'

DC Mitchell leaned forward, lowering her voice. 'No. What I'm saying is that, contrary to what you tell us, Michael was not with you when you went to the park yesterday.'

'Of course he was. Where else would he have been?'

'That's what we'd like to find out, Angie. That's one of the reasons why we are here.'

Bliss was glad they had reached the nub of it. His colleague's investigation had focussed on the missing boy rather than his mother. The single piece of identification in her bag was a debit card in the name of A. Borthwick. In the limited time available to her, Mitchell had struggled to locate details for an Angie or Angela Lawson or Borthwick anywhere in the borough. On the other hand, the CCTV footage had immediately provided her with a different slant on the case. The DC's initial concern was that the woman had perhaps abducted and harmed a child, but with no reports coming in overnight she was left to ponder the many permutations.

'I remember now,' Lawson said, adamant this time. 'Mikey was in the buggy yesterday morning because he was sleepy. I did push him there. Sorry, I forgot about that.'

'In which case,' Bliss said, 'why, when our cameras get a clear and clean view into the buggy, is it empty? Can you explain that for us, Angie? And while you're at it, my colleague here looked at previous footage going back a few days. The last time you visited the park pushing the buggy, Michael wasn't with you then, either.'

The woman blinked. 'He was. Of course he was. He must have been. With his father being away, I'm the only one Mikey has to take care of him. I'd never leave my boy at home while I went for a walk in the park. Is that what you think happened? Are you accusing me of neglecting my son?'

Bliss had a moment of inspiration. 'Please, calm yourself down, Angie. That's not what we're saying at all. Look, let's take a breath and shift back to safer ground. You've told us Michael is five years old. How old are you, if you don't me asking?'

She gave a begrudging shrug. 'It's just middle-age women who mind answering that question. I'm twenty in a couple of months.'

'So, you're nineteen now,' Bliss said, nodding gently as he absorbed the answer. 'Which means you were, what, fourteen when you had Michael?'

'Of course not,' Lawson scoffed, a deep frown creasing her brow. 'What do you take me for? Some kind of easy slag? I was nineteen when Mikey was born.'

Bliss took a long breath. He looked across at both DC Mitchell and Mr Yarwood. Both wore puzzled expressions, though the psychiatric specialist's was more one of interest than concern.

'Angie,' Yarwood said softly. He had remained standing, but now he crouched down on his haunches to bring himself to eye level with the woman. 'So far you've told us that Michael is five, and that he was born when you were nineteen – the same age you tell us you are now. You've also told these officers that your son was born in 1964, and referred to your son as a toddler.'

Lawson looked from face to face. 'Yeah? And?'

'Angie, not all of that can be equally true. Do you understand?'

'I don't know what you mean. Why are you trying to confuse me? I want to see my son. Where's Mikey? I want to see him now.'

'What year is this, Angie?' Bliss asked, deciding that as the woman had started to unravel, he might as well tease as much out of her as possible.

She regarded him as if he were dense. 'Year? What kind of question is that?'

'The simple kind. Tell me what year it is and we can be done with this.'

After a vacant pause, Lawson lowered her head and shook it slowly. 'No. I'm not answering any more of your questions. You're trying to trick me.'

'I'm really not, Angie. I have no reason to. Just looking to summarise what you've told us so far, and your answer will help me with that. Which, in turn, will also help you.'

She sighed. Looked up to meet his even gaze. Her cheeks were drawn and hollow. 'It's 1991. May 1991, to be precise. John Major is Prime Minister, and the Beatles are number one in the charts.'

Bliss noted the error at the end but nodded and smiled, anyway. 'Good. That's correct. And your son is now five, which means he was born in what year?'

'I do know what year Mikey was born. I ought to: I was there at the time.'

'That should make it easier for you to tell me when it was.'

'February. 1964.'

'Okay. And how many years between 1964 and 1991, Angie?'

The vacant look was back. As far as Bliss could tell, the woman seemed to lose herself completely in the moment. He could only guess at the thoughts running through her head, the distortions fascinating him and fuelling his dread at the same time. What was clear to him, however, was that Angie had suffered a traumatic incident at some point.

More than likely the loss of her son.

More than likely when he was five.

More than likely twenty-two years ago in 1969.

For this poor woman, time had not partially stood still during the summer of love, but rather the summer of loss.

'I think we should end it there,' Mr Yarwood said in that gentle tone of his.

Both Bliss and Mitchell nodded silently.

There was nothing more to say.

TEN

H E AND HAZEL ATE out that evening. Bliss was feeling restless and needed to take his mind off the meeting with his fellow Beatles arranged for later, as well as the poor woman currently residing at Mile End hospital in a state of mental confusion.

It was Hazel's turn to choose, so they went for Italian. He fancied a nice Madras, but Hazel wasn't particularly fond of spicy foods. Normally, the lack of a shared love of Indian cuisine was a deal breaker for Bliss, but he had pushed past that. He could always go out with his friends for a ruby, and at least these days doing so never led to trouble.

As a teenager, he and his mates had occasionally done a runner having not paid the bill after eating their curry. They weren't stupid enough to do so locally, but one night he arrived home after an eat-and-run in Chingford to discover his father on the warpath. A waiter had recognised Jimmy, and reported the incident to the police, identifying him as the son of sergeant Dennis Bliss.

'Do you know what kind of position you've put me in?' his father said to him, face taut with fury.

Bliss remembered hanging his head in shame.

'I realise it's not the crime of the century, Jimmy, but I'm a copper and it reflects badly on me if you get yourself into trouble.'

Being sixteen or seventeen at the time, Bliss had no handle on his anger. Though mortified at sullying his father's good name, his temper got the better of him. 'You're one to talk. How often do you come home from the boozer without some hooky gear? And you never question where I get hold of my films and records.'

'I take responsibility for my own actions,' Dennis Bliss said. 'I know that what I do allows us to carry on living in this house in the knowledge that we're secure, that no face in this neighbourhood is going to try it on with any of us. It keeps me grounded in the community, and that way I can sort the chancers from the hardened villains. I have no dealings with their kind, and never will have.'

'Yeah, you keep telling yourself that, dad. Bent is bent.'

This was the first and only time Jimmy Bliss ever felt fear when looking in his father's eyes. The glimmer of disappointment was hard enough to take, but when it became pure, undiluted rage, he knew he'd pushed too far.

His father stabbed a finger in his direction. 'Don't you dare use that word and me in the same sentence again. You hear me, boy? I know what I am. I might have to play the game to earn respect from the toe-rags around here, but I think I've earned it from you. There's a difference between doing what needs to be done to fit in, and being truly bent. I've never taken a back-hander in my life, I've never provided a face with information in my life, and you will never see me do a deal with the genuine scumbags who ply their trade all around us. You ever set me alongside those kind of people again, those kind of coppers again, and me and you are going to fall out in a big way.'

Chastened by the heated discussion, Bliss reacted like most teenagers by turning away in a huff. But after he had cooled down, he sought out his father to apologise. It was heartfelt, and the old man had accepted with his usual good grace. However, Bliss had always felt a bit of distance between them after that. Nothing so wide as to break the bond between father and son, merely a fissure through which a chill occasionally blew.

As he came back into the here and now, Bliss realised he had never skipped a bill at an Italian restaurant before. He didn't think now was the right time to lose his cherry.

The food was good, and Hazel looked amazing. She wore a floral dress that showed off her terrific legs to their best effect. It didn't bother him that she turned heads. He was proud and astonished to have this wonderful young woman spending time with him. A woman who wanted to live with him, to marry him eventually. Hazel had never mentioned wanting children, though. Perhaps it was too early in their relationship for that, but privately he hoped that conversation would never come. He didn't want kids, had no paternal instincts so far as he could tell, and he didn't think he would make a good father. His temper often clouded his judgement, and you had to be both willing and also keen to share your time with children if you brought them into the world. Bliss considered himself to be too selfish in that regard.

As they ate, he caught himself admiring his girlfriend. She had no idea how beautiful she was, and although she was aware of the effect her body had on him and other men, she never once flaunted her appeal. There was no sultry swing of the hips as she walked, no sticking her chest out, or angling her legs perfectly to show off the curve of her calf muscles. She wore what she liked when she liked, walked with a natural grace oozing femininity, but without any self-awareness. One of the first things he had come to understand about Hazel was that you took her as you found her, or you did not take her at all.

Bliss wanted to. At least until she tired of him, which he thought was inevitable. Maybe that was why she never mentioned children. An engagement was a relatively simply thing to quit on, a marriage less so but still something deemed acceptable if the relationship wasn't working out. Having children, on the other hand, was a different matter entirely. That came with its own set of standards and responsibilities.

He asked about her day, and listened with care as she enthused over the Sony device she had mentioned during their Friday night dinner. He didn't understand technology, let alone information technology as it was known. If he had to use any form of electronic or mechanical device, he did as little as was necessary to complete a task. Hazel had a grasp on it all, however, though her job was to advertise the product rather than be an accomplished user. She had previously explained to him that for her to truly believe in an item, she had to fully immerse herself in it first. That's what separated her from her peers, and kept her ahead of the game.

Hazel asked about his job, knowing the response would be limited. Bliss did not like to bring his work home with him, and definitely not into his relationship with her. He sensed it was the source of some frustration on her part, but he also knew that she understood and would never press him beyond that which he chose to share.

The undercover job was something he refused to mention. Although it consumed a fair amount of his time, he had decided from the outset that being aware of it would worry Hazel unduly. She would not understand his confidence, given he was stepping into the role of the very kind of person he was supposed to hunt down. He saw no good reason to give her cause for concern, because even if he didn't mention weapons she would automatically connect a robbery with guns and immediately become fearful of what might happen to him.

He did reveal a little of the investigation into the woman known to the police as Angie Lawson. DC Mitchell had carried out checks on the electoral roll, deeds and land registry, local authority housing lists, and was leaving private landlord lettings for another day. She had also made an application to Barclays bank who'd issued the woman's debit card in a different name, though neither of them fancied her chances there. A thorough search of the woman's bag had not yielded anything containing her address, nor any other useful information. Similarly, Mitchell found no record of

Michael Lawson ever having existed. A side pocket contained two keys on a ring attached to a well-worn leather fob; house keys, she assumed.

Thinking about that poor traumatised woman began to bring Bliss's mood down, so instead he spoke about his boss and how they were at loggerheads. The thought cheered him because he felt he had won a minor victory earlier in the day. When he mentioned DC Mitchell's kindness and demonstration of solidarity, he caught Hazel's curious smile.

'No,' he said, shaking his head. 'It's nothing like that. I realise that's the second time I've mentioned her now, but Faith and I are just colleagues. She sees what a hard time Moody and a handful of his cronies give me, and she lets them know I have support. That's all.'

'I don't mind,' Hazel told him. 'Even if there is something between you two. What you and I have is stronger, and always will be.'

'So if she and I had a quickie in the supply cupboard, it wouldn't bother you?'

'If she so much as gives you a wank without my permission, I'll chop her bloody hand off.'

Hearing Hazel utter words like that in an accent designed to read the BBC news brought to mind a stark image of Angela Rippon effing and jeffing. He laughed and spread his hands. 'But you just said you didn't mind because what we had was so strong.'

'It's a different matter entirely if I approve first, of course. But it doesn't bother me if you flirt a bit. You are a flirt, and I'm not about to try to change you.'

'Am I? I'd never thought of myself that way before.'

'That's because it comes naturally to you. Deep down you're a bit shy and insecure, so to overcome that you put on a front. You've been doing that for so long now that it's become a part of who you are.'

'Me? No, you're crazy.'

'Not at all. You laugh and joke with women in the same way as you do with your mates. With them it's you being friendly and dicking around, but with women they see it as you flirting with them. You make us laugh, Jimmy, and believe me that can be intoxicating.'

'So, that's why you're with me, is it? You're drunk on my wit and charm.'

Hazel laughed. 'Well, it's not your good looks or earning potential. You're no Richard Gere, and I doubt you'll ever be able to buy me a Merc for our anniversary. Be thankful for your personality and hang on for dear life. Me and you... we're going to be one wild ride together.'

He joined in with her laughter, wondering precisely what she had meant when she mentioned giving her approval.

ELEVEN

THE MEETING TOOK PLACE on a pedestrian bridge overlooking the industrial estate they would be hitting on Friday night. From their position, they could see most of the area unfolding beneath them. It was the first time all four of the Beatles had surveyed the site together, and it was Bliss who mentioned how busy the roads going in and out of the estate were.

Seemingly unconcerned, John shrugged. 'We're not after a fast getaway here. We'll be driving out at the same speed as we drive in. Remember, at best they won't know they've been hit until they go to unload the safe in preparation for the Securicor van. Worst case is they somehow discover it as soon as they return to the office, which still gives us a ten-to-fifteen-minute head start. We'll be well on the way to Woodford by the time they raise the alarm, and even then the filth will be looking for a fire services motor with different plates.'

Bliss nodded. Stripping the magnetic livery markers off the van and swapping out the number plates before they left the estate meant the store manager would describe entirely the wrong vehicle when he reported the theft.

'It's all down to you, George,' John said, narrowing his gaze. 'The plan works. The timing works. Ringo assures me his device is foolproof. The one thing that can go wrong now is if you can't open that safe inside ten minutes. That gives us five to empty it. Any longer and the manager gets suspicious.'

'Don't worry about me. I won't need five of those minutes. I know those safes better than I do the back of my hand. I told you before, if one of the default combinations doesn't work, I can crack the thing wide open within ten attempts.'

'That's what I like. Confidence.'

'It's my living, John. It's how you came to hear of me.'

'It was my brother who came up with your name. To be honest with you, I was all for using somebody known to us for what is, after all, the most important part of the job. But as was pointed out to me, the three blokes I had in mind had all done some bird at one time or another, which meant they'd all been caught at some point in their careers. You never have.'

'And I don't intend to start now.'

Paul had been listening closely. He turned to George and said, 'So are you really that good, or are you that lucky?'

'Does it matter, provided I don't get pinched for it?'

'Yeah. Because luck runs out eventually.'

Bliss smiled. 'Just as well for you I'm that good, then.'

All four of them chuckled at that. The strange thing was, Bliss enjoyed their company. John, Paul and Ringo were criminals, so he had no qualms with the notion of them being banged up after the job. He would feel nothing for any of them when that happened. But right here, right now, before this crime was due to be committed, they were four men talking and having a laugh to rid themselves of nervous tension. The Beatles on a night out. A hard day's night, maybe.

'You got one or two alternative routes out of here?' Ringo asked him. 'Just in case of a pile-up blocking the road.'

'Of course. Plans B, C, and D. You don't have to worry about me.'

'I do,' John said. 'I have to worry about all of you. Any one of you fucks up and we have problems.'

'I get it. I do. But we're cool. So, let me ask you something. After we pull this off, do we stick together as a team and do another job?'

'Why d'you ask?'

'Because this isn't your first rodeo, yet you've come into it with a completely new crew. That makes me wonder what happened to your previous one.'

'Maybe you shouldn't be so interested in the past. Keep your mind on the here and now.'

'You might be right, but all the same… I'm asking.'

John turned square on to him. 'And if I don't feel like telling you? If I say it's none of your fucking business?'

Bliss thought about the best course of action. As a copper he knew this was the time to take a step back, to not challenge the man's authority. But he asked himself how the villain he was playing might react. A like-minded criminal would be reluctant to show weakness at this point.

'I'm still asking,' he said. 'And I want an answer. Because either your last crew were nicked, which would concern me, or you decided not to use them again, which also bothers me. So, I think it is my business.'

Without any obvious movement, Bliss angled his body slightly and dragged a foot backwards to stabilise his stance. Declan O'Shea had a reputation as a hot head, and when he turned it was rapid and fierce. Bliss did not fancy his chances against the man, but if the gangster launched himself, Bliss was determined to get in the first blow.

Ringo cut the tension. 'As it goes, John, George here has a point. I was wondering the same thing. I know you never promised any long-term commitment, but it would be good to know if this is a one-off or if there's more work on the go afterwards.'

John drew himself up to his full height. For a moment, Bliss was certain punches were about to be thrown. Instead, the man shrugged. 'Don't worry yourselves about previous crews. Nobody got caught, nobody is doing bird for a job they did with me. The truth is, we never do more than half a dozen jobs with the same crew. It breeds familiarity, and a team loses its edge when that happens. Also, the longer a crew spends together, the more likely it is that some bloody copper will turn them. So we switch things out as and when we see fit. You asked for an answer, and there you have it.'

It was good enough for Bliss, but he debated pushing it further. This was the last scheduled meeting ahead of the job, and having asked his bosses for more elbow room, he wanted to use them now. 'Fair enough, John,' he said. 'I appreciate your honesty. One more thing… since you happened to mention it the other day, will we get introduced to your boss at any point?'

'He's not my fucking boss,' John snarled. 'I don't answer to him, and neither does my brother. He's just a fellah who puts things together from time to time and takes a fee for his troubles, that's all.'

Bliss held his hands up defensively. 'All right, pal. No need to get lairy. You made it sound as if he was somebody you answered to, that's all. It's no skin off my nose either way. I was just wondering if we were going to meet him.'

'You're suddenly all about the questions, aren't you, Georgie boy? You don't say boo to a fucking goose all this time, and now today you want to know the ins and outs of a duck's arse. What's that all about?'

'You'll be suggesting I swan about next.'

'What?'

'Nothing. I like to know who I'm working for and how that might pan out in the future. I've held my tongue until now because I hoped you'd be a bit more forthcoming. You didn't seem inclined to tell us anything beyond what we needed to know for this one job, so I brought it up. No big deal.'

'Yeah, well I'm still wondering why you've suddenly become a real nosy bastard today. I don't like change, George. Especially on top of bumping into you the other night in a boozer far away from where you kip down.'

This caught the attention of Paul, who until now had stayed out of the argument. 'Oh, yeah. What was all that about? We're not supposed to meet in public ahead of the job.'

John nodded, and Bliss felt the full force of his stern gaze. 'I went to meet with a fellah for a drink over Bethnal Green way. And who do I see sitting there in the boozer with some tart, but our very own Beatle here.'

Paul raised his eyebrows. 'Some tart, eh?'

Bliss felt heat prickling his flesh. 'Don't call her that. There's no need.'

'No offence,' John said, 'but the way she was dressed... looked like she was on the game to me, Georgie boy.'

Bliss wanted to hit him. There was a time not so long ago that he would have, without needing to think twice. But that would put an end to the job, and possibly his career. He didn't want that, but he didn't want this, either. He had to stop it before things got out of hand.

'Look, no matter what she is or isn't, she's still a friend. There's no need to talk her down. What I told you is the truth, John. We were friends growing up. She moved away from the area, but we kept in touch. Yeah, she's a brass, but I don't like to hear people talk about her like that.'

The big man held up a hand. 'Like I said, no offence. You're a lucky man to have a friend like her. If that's all you two are.'

'It is.'

'Nobody expects you to live like a monk. If you're getting your leg over that and not having to pay for it, I'd say you've done well there.'

Bliss started to feel a familiar heat rising. He set his jaw before responding. 'We're friends. I suggest you leave it there. Maybe this is all banter to you, but where I come from we don't talk about friends that way.'

'And where exactly do you come from, Georgie? That's what I'd like to know.'

'You know as much as I need people like you to know. The rest protects me from getting my collar felt. Move on, John. This won't end well otherwise.'

John shrugged. 'I can do that. By the way, as you were leaving, I asked the barman if he recognised the pair of you. He told me he'd seen the tar… the girl in there before. He didn't get a good look at you, so couldn't be sure. Said you might be familiar.'

Bliss felt like breathing a sigh of relief. Had the barman got a good look at him he might have spoken without thinking it through – the staff knew what kind of place it was, and didn't offer information to relative strangers.

'I wouldn't have thought so, as it goes. I've only ever been in there a couple of times before.'

'Is that all? Strange, seeing as you and her are such close friends.'

'Look, what the fuck is this? Why are you banging on about it?'

'No reason, Georgie boy. I just find it a little bit suspicious, is all.'

Bliss stood his ground. 'Of what? What are you not saying?'

John clearly wasn't prepared to take a backward step, either. 'When people want to know more than I'm ready to tell them, then I want to know more about their reasons for wanting to know more. And when it comes on top of me seeing them out of place, my mind gets to spinning its wheels. You get that, right?'

'Just about. But let me be clear, John. If you don't trust me, if you think there's something sussy about me, I can always walk away if that puts your mind at rest. I'm not happy being called out for no good reason, make no mistake about that. To be honest, you three all seem decent enough blokes, but I don't like not knowing who is running the show behind the scenes. I keep thinking of some geezer pulling levers on the other side of a green curtain, and I ain't happy about it.'

He breathed out. Heavily. Had he gone too far? Looking at John's wide-eyed face, he thought he was about to find out.

'Don't be so fucking touchy,' John said, though his gaze was far from friendly. 'This trust thing runs both ways, I get that. You don't have to concern yourself, that's all I'm saying. After the job, I'll be shooting off to give your man his share, and then we're done with him until he comes through with something else.'

'But he's not *my* man, is he? He's yours.'

'It's an expression, for fuck's sake. You never dealt with an Irishman before, George?'

'I know it's an expression. I was making a point.'

'Stuff your point. Look, I can use you fellahs between this job and the next one we get from your man, so we'll set something up. Me and Dermot always have irons in the fire. Be patient, and let's get through this first bloody job. Okay?'

Bliss nodded. He had everything he needed; there was no need to push further.

'Good man.' John clapped him on the upper arm, a chilling grin splitting his solid plank of face. 'One final thing. Sorry, but I can't let it go unsaid. George, I respect you for standing up for yourself and your friend. I'm sure she's a lovely girl. But you ever come back at me like that again and I'll forget what a gentle giant I am. Understood?'

Bliss dropped his gaze. It was time to withdraw. 'Yeah. Understood. You're the boss, John. I needed to know where things stood, and now I do.'

'All right. Well unless one of you other eejits has something else to say, let's get the fuck out of here. Same time Thursday night for phone calls, lads. If we don't talk then walk, because it means the job isn't on.'

'What happens afterwards if it goes that way?' Ringo asked.

'You'll either hear from me or you won't.'

That wasn't the response any of them wanted, but the ensuing silence clearly suggested none of them were about to provoke John into action. The man was running hot, and Bliss headed back to his car wondering if he had blown it after all.

TWELVE

AFTER A QUIET DRINK alone, during which Bliss gathered his thoughts, he drove to his temporary home in Church Road, Leyton. The police safe house had been redeveloped into separate flats, one of which was set up as the rented home of Vincent Styles. When Bliss approached the three-storey house, he was about to put his Yale key in the lock when he noticed the front door was ajar. In a shared house this was not necessarily unusual, but he knew the two remaining flats were not currently in use.

Bliss took a step back. Beyond the mottled glass panels of the door the hallway was in darkness, and he had no way of knowing whether whoever had forced their way into the house was still inside. His first instinct was to suspect burglars, but he also wondered whether this had anything to do with the role he was playing.

He walked back along the front path and looked up and down the street. Lights glowed from the windows of the fire station, and beyond that the series of looming tower blocks on the Oliver Close estate. There was no movement on the pavements, but sparse traffic shifted in both directions. It was a main road and cars seldom parked on its double yellow lines. Seeing nothing close by, Bliss jogged down to the closest junction.

He squinted in the darkness, searching for signs of life in one of the parked vehicles, or misted glass which would tell him a car had at least one occupant. The Ford Sierra RS Cosworth provided to him for the undercover job sat yards away, its engine still ticking as it cooled. He saw nothing along the street to concern him, so headed back to the house.

When he nudged the door open, Bliss winced at the sound of its hinges squealing like an aged crypt door. He stepped into the passageway and flipped the switch on the wall. The hall immediately flooded with light, and he was relieved to find nobody waiting for him. He looked further into the distance and saw the door to his flat lying wide open. It was hard to get past his instinctive reaction to call for backup, but he had to. Here he was Vincent Styles, safecracker and getaway driver, not Jimmy Bliss, Detective Constable.

He swallowed once and stomped along the passage-way, balling his hands into tight fists. 'I don't know who the fuck you think you are in my gaff!' he called out, injecting the full weight of his anger. 'But you picked the wrong fucking place to burgle tonight.'

Bursting into his flat, he switched on the lights and quickly went from room to room, looking inside his wardrobe, under the bed, and in the airing cupboard. He checked the double doors leading out to the back garden, but they were undamaged and locked. Who-ever had broken in was gone, but as he surveyed the flat, Bliss was only partially reassured.

He had worked enough burglary inquiries to know the difference between a ransacked property and one that had merely been searched. This was clearly the latter, and the thought squeezed his insides. He had nothing of value here, and as with the Cosworth, the TV, stereo and VHS recorder/player had all been sup-plied by his CID undercover unit. The electronic items were all still in place, but the flat had been turned over in a methodical search for something.

Bliss's gut clenched. This had to be the work of somebody close to Declan O'Shea. Perhaps even his brother. Either way, it now seemed likely that O'Shea had been spooked enough by catching his fellow Beatle with Elaine in the pub on Monday night, and had subsequently ordered the search to coincide with the scheduled meeting overlooking Friday's target. No wonder the big man had been so on edge. This explained the mood and the reaction to Bliss's questions.

Jimmy was certain they could not have stumbled across any incriminating evidence. Every facet of his cover had been worked on to stand up to rigorous scrutiny, including this precise circumstance. Bliss never brought anything personal into the flat, so all the documentation and financial evidence stuffed away inside drawers pointed to Vincent Styles having rented the flat for the past eighteen months.

Bliss went across to the long sideboard containing four of those drawers plus two cupboards. Everything was still where he expected to find it, though it was obvious to him that somebody had rifled through it. The rental book from his supposed landlord was crumpled, but all the pages were intact. He had no separate electricity, gas or water bills as they were included in the rent as per his agreement letter, which had been lying beneath the card itself. A recent British Telecom phone bill tied a landline to this address in Vincent's name. And finally, should he have reason to display it, there was even a passport bearing his photo in the name of Vincent Styles.

Anybody leaving this flat having searched it thoroughly would be left in no doubt that this was where

Vincent – aka George – lived. The one question that remained was who was Vincent Styles.

The legend had been created in the mid-eighties. In the same way that some criminals obtained a different identity, so the police had followed suit. The real Vincent Styles had died at the age of four following complications arising from meningitis. It had been a simple enough task for CID to resurrect him while at the same time obscuring any record of his death. Parental and sibling links had been fabricated to present Vincent as a boy who had come through the care system, striking out on his own the moment the state stopped being responsible for him. It was a well-worn path for fake identities, and made life simple for anybody taking on the persona. The fewer ties to the past, the less chance you had of blowing your cover.

Bliss slumped down onto his sofa, examining and reflecting upon what had happened. That O'Shea had scratched an itch was no big deal – Jimmy would have done the exact same thing in the man's shoes. Only a fool would ignore something if they thought it suspicious, and the O'Shea brothers were anything but foolish. This had their stamp all over it. The real question was whether they were now satisfied with what they had discovered.

As Tuesday ticked over into Wednesday, he decided to wait until his shift to inform the team. The way he saw it, if he was suspected of anything, he would probably have arrived home to more than an empty flat. A beating, possibly worse, would have awaited him. His best guess was he was in the clear. Whether the search had fully allayed their suspicions, Bliss reckoned he would find out soon enough.

Come Thursday night, he would be waiting by the phone as instructed. If the call didn't come, he'd know his cover was considered suspect, if not fully blown. If it did, he'd either be walking into a trap on Friday night or he'd be taking part in a robbery. All in all, these were strange days, Bliss thought. Strange days indeed.

Which was when he felt a movement behind him and something being looped around his neck. He barely had a chance to react when the cord pulled tight against his throat. Bliss felt himself start to choke, gagging for air, his hands scrambling wildly for purchase to prevent whoever was strangling him from completing their job.

But neither momentum nor leverage was with him, and as his vision fogged and his head started to spin, Bliss realised he was not in control of whether he lived or died. Before the full weight of darkness descended upon him, he found time to think about Hazel and the regrets he had over not already asking her to marry him.

THIRTEEN

THE FIRST THING BLISS did every working morning after sleeping at the Leyton flat was to return the car. His station had their own small yard for storage and repairs, but the main larger complex used by several nicks in the area backed onto the railway line at the Limehouse Basin. There he left the Sierra and drove away again in his own Vauxhall Cavalier, swapping Vincent Styles for Jimmy Bliss in the process. It was a tiresome routine, but one he had not yet neglected. He knew the potential danger associated with him accidentally pulling up to collect Hazel or outside his parents' house in the Cosworth, and he had a cover story prepared in case he slipped up. It was something he would rather not have to lie his way out of, so he maintained his focus.

On those nights when he stayed at the flat, people close to him made assumptions. He reckoned his father had a rough idea of what was going on, but his mother assumed he was either at Hazel's place or sleeping on a friend's settee. His girlfriend hopefully didn't concern herself with his whereabouts at all. His was a precarious existence, and one he'd already decided he would prefer not to repeat in the future. He knew of officers who went deep, fully immersing themselves in their legend, living the life twenty-four hours a day. It was not for him, especially with his relationship with Hazel still so relatively fresh and full of possibilities.

Bliss had clawed himself out of temporary uncon- sciousness shortly after being choked out. The moment he realised he was alive, his hands went to his throat but found no cord. His skin was tender to the touch, and when he checked in the bathroom mirror he saw a collar of rough, red welts. Over several cups of tea he asked himself why he wasn't dead. The conclusion he reached was that his arrival home had disturbed whoever had broken in, at which point they must have secreted themselves behind the sofa. The choking had been applied to put him out of action temporarily, not to cause any lasting harm. All of which told him he'd been right all along: the O'Shea brothers were suspi- cious, had checked up on him, and he had survived because they found nothing to back up their suspicions and still needed him for the safe on Friday night.

Having showered and shaved, Bliss studied the chafed weals around his neck. Whatever had been used on him had been rough, which told him more that he wished to dwell upon. He had nothing like that lying around in the flat, so whoever had broken in had brought the cord with them. That meant one thing: if they had found any evidence suggesting he was someone other than Vincent Styles, their intention had been to kill him. Bliss made a mental note to thank the team who'd put together the legend and the documentation that went with it.

At the station that morning he immediately sought out DCI England. Moody would probably have another pop at him for not taking his concerns to him first, but the undercover operation fell within the Chief Inspector's oversight, and this was rightfully his information to disclose to others as and when he thought best.

Bliss walked England through the awkward few minutes inside the pub when O'Shea had spotted him and Elaine, followed by the strained meeting close to the warehouse, and finally the discovery of the break-in and the resulting physical attack. The DCI made notes as Bliss talked, but did not interrupt. He was a man who considered everything in great detail before weighing in with his opinions.

'Let's take this in some kind of chronological order, DC Bliss,' England said when he was finished telling his story. 'We'll begin with this Elaine woman. She's a snout of yours, correct?'

'Yes, sir.'

'Registered?'

'Yes, she is.'

'Had you arranged to see her that night?'

Bliss knew why he'd been asked that particular question. 'No, sir. If you're wondering if Elaine is somehow involved and tipped off O'Shea, that's not the case. We bumped into each other purely by chance. It's not a pub I use on a regular basis, and when she and I meet we do so far away from public scrutiny. She went in for a drink, spotted me and came over for a chat. It was all perfectly innocent. She'd not been there long when Declan O'Shea came in.'

England glanced down at one of the notes he had made. 'You don't think O'Shea might have been onto her rather than you? As your informant, I mean. You definitely didn't get the impression that he had followed her there?'

Bliss had to think about that one before replying. It was something he had not previously considered. 'I can't be certain, sir, but I'm confident that what I saw on O'Shea's face was surprise at seeing me sitting there, laced with a bit of suspicion that crept in as an afterthought. I'm just as confident – if not more so – that he had no idea who Elaine was.'

'Okay. Not as categorical as I'd like, but let's go with your gut for now. So, onto the meeting. It went well otherwise?'

'It did. We ran it through and it was good to see the place up close rather than on a map. I've driven past the estate a few times, but never taken a great deal of notice of it before.'

'Then O'Shea brought up the subject of seeing you in the pub.'

Bliss bit into his lip. Eventually he shrugged and said, 'I think that's on me, sir. I asked a couple of questions too many for his liking. I should have known better, but I wanted to get a feel for who this mysterious Mr Big might be. That's when Declan quizzed me about Elaine and my being in the pub.'

'But you think he bought your explanation at the time, that you two were ex-neighbours and close friends?'

'Yes, sir. Elaine was sharp and she played it just right. She knew it was an iffy situation. For her as well, considering she's my snout. She wouldn't have wanted that to get out.'

'Quite so.' DCI England nodded, checking his notes again. 'You didn't see who he was there to meet, and you got out of there fast. I think that was for the best.

Hanging around might have aroused his suspicions all the more. Right, so next we come to what you found when you arrived home. I agree with your assessment. If O'Shea suspected you of something, if he was unsure about you in any way, searching your home and establishing your credentials was the most logical next step. As to that, I have full confidence in the legend, and there's every chance the brothers would have felt a good deal better about you afterwards. I think we should look upon it as a positive thing.'

'Excluding the fact they choked me out?'

The DCI grinned. 'Indeed. And again, I have to agree with your own conclusions on that matter. The intention was to incapacitate you so that whoever broke in could slip away again.'

Bliss automatically put a hand to his throat, now covered by a collar and tie. 'I definitely think we have to assume that's the case, yes, sir.'

'Then despite your alarm and discomfort, it augers well for the job going ahead.'

'That's precisely what I was thinking as I drove in this morning, sir. I may have given Declan a few doubts, but the takeaway from what happened in my flat would have been that I am who I say I am, and Vincent Styles has a reputation for coming through.'

'The officer who had the job before you worked for three gangs in all. It was too good a legend to burn, so we've taken no action against any of them so far. What it did was give us an inside presence and more intelligence than we can possibly ever use. It told us where to place the deep cover men if we decided to go that way, or it gave us other methods of keeping tabs on these gangs. If the O'Sheas go to any of them for a reference, it'll be a blinder.'

'And you're absolutely certain there are no photographs?'

'We don't believe so, no.'

'In which case, the biggest danger to me is still the O'Sheas having someone on the inside here.'

England nodded. 'It is. Sadly. But that is always the risk, Constable. You knew that going in.'

'I understand that, sir. I've come to terms with it, and I don't think I'd have come this far with them if that was the case. Like you suggested, Declan and Dermot will probably be happier with me today than they have been at any time since they first called me in.'

'So we're still a go, then?'

Bliss gave an emphatic nod. 'Of course. Tomorrow night I need the getaway cars driven over to the estate where I'm supposed to be keeping them after they've been nicked. The non-brand keys will be left inside the exhaust pipes for me and Ringo. Apart from that and knowing the safe combination, I'm as ready as I'll ever be.'

'Good man. I'll have a word with DI Moody. I'll update him on everything we have discussed, but suggest he leave you be so that you can prepare yourself fully for Friday night. Which reminds me, the store manager called first thing. This week's code for the safe is L30-R07-L19-R66.'

Bliss frowned. The numbers seemed familiar to him. Then he smiled as he realised what it was. 'The date England lifted the World Cup, sir. Memorable. To us football fans, at least.'

DCI England seemed unimpressed. 'I'm more of a summer sport man myself. Cricket and tennis, you know? Bit of golf. Still, it's good that you'll be able to keep it inside your head. We wouldn't get far without it, would we?'

Bliss laughed. It was the one sure thing about this entire venture. The one thing he knew could not possibly go wrong.

FOURTEEN

MOODY WAS LIVING UP to his name and keeping out of everybody's way by remaining in his office with the window blinds drawn. Rumour had it that he'd recently caught his wife having a bit on the side, but Bliss thought the Inspector's malaise went deeper than that. His nose had been put out of joint over the planning of the undercover sting, and he was most assuredly sitting alone nursing discontent and resentment.

To take his mind off the Beatles and the warehouse raid, Bliss threw himself into helping DC Mitchell with her investigation. They took themselves off into a quiet office populated by a young uniformed constable whose speciality lay in getting the most out of the now legendary woeful computer database.

The Police National Computer system comprised several databases, all interlinked, making searches relating to criminal behaviour, vehicle-related incidents, and both stolen and found property. A relatively simple task in the hands of somebody who knew the correct syntax when querying its records. None of which helped their cause when investigating Angie Lawson's background, as far as Bliss could see. Using either surname associated with the woman, they quickly discovered no criminal record, no driving licence, and she had never reported being the victim of a burglary or street theft.

The way Faith Mitchell thought about computer bods, she reckoned there was a good chance that those who spoke the same language sought one another out, or at the very least welcomed contact from like-minded specialists. PC Douglas Fleet swiftly absorbed what he was being asked for, yet when the DC was finished with her explanation, shook his head and shrugged.

'I understand what it is you're after,' he said. 'But in order to find the right answer, you have to ask precisely the right question. It's not like in real life when you ask something in general terms and the person you ask gets the broader gist. Computers can't think like that. They are literal. So the question becomes the most important thing of all.'

'What's the bloody point of them if they can't help in a crisis?' Bliss said, frustrated at being given the cold shoulder by the system he and his colleagues had been ordered to embrace.

Fleet smiled. Humouring him. 'Think of it this way, DC Bliss. With the old methods, you begin with a filing cabinet. Inside each drawer are numerous files. If, say, you wanted to know which females under the age of fifty stole cash from a pensioner last year, you would have to wade through those files and pull out all robbery offences from 1990. Then you would have to sift through them to remove only those relating to females, and from that pile take out those whose age did not fit the parameters... and so on. Think of how long that would take you with a paper-based system. With a database, I can key in specific searches to cover every one of those case aspects. It would take me a minute or two at most. The result would be spat out in half that time.'

'Which all sounds extremely impressive, Constable Fleet, but it doesn't seem to be able to tell me who this woman is and whether she ever had a child called Michael.'

'Which is where we come back to asking the right questions.'

Bliss folded his arms. 'Which are?'

'Begin with what you know. Then identify what you don't know. This will leave you with the blanks that need filling in.'

'I don't need a bloody computer to tell me that, nor a sodding computer whizz.' He tapped the side of his head. 'Sound logic and astute reasoning told me the same thing hours ago.'

'Ah, let me finish. Once you have that information, you look at which computer systems best suits your needs. If they even exist. Let me demonstrate what I mean. Tell me one thing you don't know for certain about this woman.'

'Her real name,' Mitchell said.

'Which will be somewhere within the OPCS records.'

'What's the OPCS when it's at home?'

'The Office of Population and Censuses Surveys. The General Register Office – which is the specific department you need – has been a part of the OPCS for about twenty years now.'

'Do you think you can get into their records? Do you know somebody who can?'

Fleet shook his head. 'Sorry, but no can do. They're not digitised.'

Bliss puffed out his cheeks. 'Well, that's a couple of minutes of my life I'm never going to get back.'

'I'm sorry, DC Bliss, but in order to identify how and where to obtain information, you must also rule out how and where you can't. Am I right?'

He was. Bliss gave a grudging nod. 'Sorry. It's a bit frustrating to hear something similar to my own thought process spelled out for me. All right, I see where we're headed with this. Let me think about records that will exist.'

'I've been through housing,' Mitchell reminded him. 'Private landlords are all I have left to check out now.'

'You'll get no joy from them,' Fleet said. 'Being private concerns they're not legally obliged to go out of their way to help without a warrant. I think we're going to have to come at this a different way. For obvious reasons, the financial institutions are most likely to keep the best records and store them on electronic databases.'

'I have a request in with Barclays bank. Angie has a debit card with them. Or, at least, we assume it's hers. It's in the name of A. Borthwick. That may well be her real name.'

'Perhaps her maiden name. Anyway, as far as they are concerned, all you've done is make a request for information on a customer, and they'll drag their heels on that. If you elevated your request to something more formal, such as the details you require being part of a criminal investigation, they're obliged to provide it to you.'

DC Mitchell looked at Bliss. He nodded. The woman sectioned at the Mile End hospital was not currently the subject of an investigation, but they both knew a swift change of language could steer things their way.

'If we obtain the authority, will you speak to a counterpart at Barclays?' Mitchell asked Fleet. 'Angie's banking records may help us, but more importantly they'll tell us where she lives.'

'And then we light the blue touch paper and stand back,' Bliss muttered. 'Because when we open up this can of worms, I think we're going to get some fireworks.'

FIFTEEN

Bliss understood the one unimpeachable fact about all women: they knew when something was wrong. Always. Throughout his childhood and youth it always felt as if his mother had either a sixth sense or was a witch. There were no other possibilities. Because it never seemed to matter how brave a face he put on anything, she would look at him with those knowing eyes that had a laser fix to his heart. And a look was often all it took to break his resolve.

Hazel had that same way about her. On Wednesday evening they went out for a drink. It was her night to choose the venue, and she asked him to meet her at the World's End pub on the corner of Stroud Green Road in Finsbury Park. It was a strange choice, but Bliss went along without quarrel.

The four-storey building had the sober look of many such old pubs in London, its dour facade not exactly welcoming; though the paintwork had at least been freshened since Bliss had last been inside. The interior was more inviting and brightly lit, and he was deep into his first pint by the time Hazel arrived. If he admired the instincts so often demonstrated by women, Bliss knew his were not too shabby, either. And the gleam in his girlfriend's eyes suggested excitement diluted by anxiety.

Please don't tell me you're pregnant, he thought. *I love you, Haze, but this is too much too soon…*

He fetched her a Malibu and lemonade, and as he set the glass on the table he asked why she had decided on this place for their night out.

'I haven't,' she said, taking a sip and grinning at him. She smacked her lips. 'I thought we'd have one here and take a walk afterwards.'

'A walk? In Finsbury Park? Leave it out, Haze. Do you know how many Gooners live around here?'

'Oh, you and your sodding football. So what if some people follow other teams… it's not the end of the world, Jimmy.'

He chuckled and made a show of looking around. 'Actually, that's exactly what this place is.'

She shook her head and rolled her eyes. 'You fool. Anyway, I didn't mean an aimless walk around the streets. The thing is, Jimmy, I think I've found us somewhere. A place of our own, I mean.'

TONY J FORDER

If he was relieved at her not announcing a pregnancy, it soon faded when he thought of moving out here. 'It's a bit of a distance, isn't it? I know I said it might be better for us to live away from where I work, but this is not what I had in mind at all.'

Hazel said nothing for a few moments, but kept her eyes on his. When she finally spoke, she did so in that calm and authoritative way of hers that he had never been able to resist. '*We* are our home. You and me. Whatever we live inside is just a shell, and wherever that shell happens to be, it's just a place. Our home is you and me and whatever we bring to it. And it's what we do inside our home that counts, not what's outside. I've actually seen this place, Jimmy, because my friend is renting it at the moment and she has the option of passing on her lease. It's a lovely flat, ground floor, with a nice little garden. Living room, diner and kitchen, bathroom, separate toilet, and a decent patio right outside the bedroom French windows. It's everything we need, and it's available at the end of the month.'

For once, Bliss had no ready answer. He could see she wanted this. Really wanted it. 'Is there room for all my albums?' he asked.

Hazel wrinkled her nose. 'I don't know about that. Even if there is, I'm not sure what the neighbours will make of it.'

'Why? What's wrong with my music?'

'There's nothing wrong with it… exactly. It's just that your tastes are so eclectic. One minute it's that Dirty Waters blues player you seem to admire, and next it's something from somebody like Boz Scaggs.'

Stifling a laugh, Bliss said, 'Well, first of all it's Muddy Waters. And secondly, I could easily go from Deep Purple to Rickie Lee Jones and then on to Miles Davis. Music is music, Haze. If my ears like it, I'll play it.'

'Oh, I know. But why can't you stick with Michael Jackson and be done with it?'

They laughed, this time together. 'It sounds nice,' he said, taking her hand in his across the table. 'The flat, I mean. Somewhere to call our own, to get us started. We can look at buying our own gaff later.'

Hazel smiled and squeezed his fingers. 'A house and a couple of dogs, maybe. You could call them Butch and Sundance. I know you love that film.'

Bliss nodded. He did, but he couldn't see himself naming a dog Sundance. Nor Butch, for that matter, given he favoured Labradors. 'We'll see. You never mentioned kids, I notice.'

Her wide smile faltered, and for a second she glanced away. Not looking elsewhere, but inside. 'I suppose the longer we stay together the more likely we are to have that conversation.'

'You're reluctant?'

'Another day, eh, Jimmy? I'm not sure I'm ready to talk in those terms just yet.'

He nodded. Her clipped tone told him to back off. Then he remembered something. When she had entered the pub he'd seen excitement shining from her face, and her news about the flat rental explained that. But she had also been anxious.

'Tell me what's troubling you?' he said. 'And don't bother denying it. You're not the only one good at reading people, you know?'

Nodding, Hazel took a deep breath and let it all out. 'There's something not quite right about you at the moment, Jimmy. It's been that way for a few weeks now, and it's starting to worry me.'

'In what way?'

'You're… reserved. But you're also behaving secretively. I realise there could be a hundred reasons for that, but I worry that it's about me and you. So before we move in together and start planning out the rest of our lives, especially a family, I need to know if you're seeing someone else.'

Bliss closed his eyes. Clearly he was not as good at hiding his emotions as he thought he was. He gripped her hand tighter still and leaned in. 'Hazel, you're the best choice I ever made. You're the best choice I will ever make. I want to spend the rest of my life with you, and for me that doesn't mean coming home to you every night as my wife, but then also sharing a bed with someone else. I love you, Haze. That means I'm all in. All the way. You're my girl. You're the one. And nothing is ever going to change that. You and me, Hazel Smith, are going to grow old together.'

SIXTEEN

Jimmy Bliss awoke on the morning of his twenty-ninth birthday with Hazel wrapped in his arms. As he picked sleep crust from his eyes and blinked to sharpen his vision, it became obvious to him that his girlfriend had been awake for some time. Her smile was brighter and warmer than the sun spearing through the gap between the curtains pulled across his bedroom's solitary window. With devilment in her feline gaze, she pecked him on the nose, then his forehead, and hugged him close.

'Morning, birthday boy,' she virtually sang. 'Now, tell me what you want first; your presents, your breakfast, or… me?'

Hazel giggled and threw back the bedclothes. She was already dressed. Partially, at least. She wore lacy black underwear and sheer black stockings, complete with suspender belt. 'I thought I'd give you something extra to unwrap this morning.'

Her body always excited him, but the way she looked at that moment took his breath away. He exhaled heavily, wondering if he would ever be able to draw another in. At times like this he could not believe his luck. He had always considered himself to be lacking academically, but was known to be a deep thinker, somehow comprehending more than he had ever knowingly learned. Hazel was more than a match for him cerebrally, which often made their conversations a joy. Given her financially comfortable, moderately Christian upbringing, Bliss had assumed when they first dated that she would be sexually repressed. He was happy to admit this was another magical example of how wrong he had been on that score. With Hazel, anything seemed to be within bounds, and there was nothing dutiful about the way she made love.

Straddling him now, her easy smile becoming lustful as she took rasping breaths, Hazel unhooked her bra and leaned forward to allow it to fall from her shoulders. Bliss sighed as he took in the beauty of her figure. Fully aroused and all sense of sleep long forgotten, he reached up to pull her close. Her own hand slid from his chest and started sliding slowly – tantalisingly – downwards.

Which was the exact moment his mother rapped her knuckles on the bedroom door. 'Breakfast is on the table,' she called out. 'Happy birthday, sweetheart. Morning, Hazel.'

'Good morning, Jacqui,' Hazel managed to reply around the hand she had stuffed over her mouth to suppress a fit of laughter.

Bliss groaned deep in the back of his throat. 'Morning, Mum.' He flopped out on the bed, pretending to weep.

'That seems to have unsettled the mood,' Hazel whispered.

'You're not kidding. Nothing like your mum's voice to throw cold water on… well, you know what it throws cold water on. And there was me thinking I was going to get the same present from you as I got for Christmas when we woke up in *your* bed.'

Hazel pouted, firming her lips. 'You should be so lucky. Those days are long gone, Jimmy. I'm a nice respectable girlfriend now, like your mummy always wanted.'

Bliss pulled the pillow out from beneath his head and whacked her with it. 'You better not be,' he told her, grinning. 'I have plans for you later.'

'In that case, I'll keep my lingerie clean.'

'Not that I need it. Not with what you look like without it.'

'Should I not bother, then?'

He leaned up on his elbows. 'Oh, I think you should. But I'm telling you now, it won't all stay on for long.'

This time he was the one who got slammed by the pillow.

Thirty minutes later, after chomping his way through a full English fry-up, he was opening presents. Hazel had bought him a silk tie in two different shades of maroon, plus two albums: *All Right Now*, which was the best of Free, and REM's new one, *Out of Time*. His parents' gift contained two VHS films, both of which had been suggested to them by Hazel. He was thrilled to see both *Pacific Heights* and *Miller's Crossing*, two films he had enjoyed enormously at the cinema. He hadn't been able to unwrap his best gift of all, but he basked in the knowledge that he had plenty of time for that. And not for only a day, either.

He thought the gift-giving was over, but then Hazel stepped out of the room and came back with a final present; this time from all three of them. It wasn't wrapped, and the shape of the case it came in was unmistakable. Excited as a schoolboy, he snapped back the latches and opened the lid. Inside was a Martin D-10 Dreadnought acoustic guitar. Bliss was an enthusiast who played regularly, but his old Yamaha had seen better days. This beauty was expensive, made from sapele wood, with a tone to die for. Almost too good to play.

Thanks were not enough, but he gave them along with hugs all round. The beautiful instrument had left him close to speechless, and he couldn't wait to spend time with it. The rest of his birthday breakfast passed by with a minimum of fuss. He was understandably on edge about the following day, and still carried some guilt with him at having to lie to everyone he knew since starting the undercover job. It had been drummed into him from the outset that absolutely nobody could know, and that included family, wives and girlfriends. His father was also excluded. Bliss accepted the instruction as the way the job had to run, because the one sure way to keep a secret was to tell nobody. Only those involved in the sting operation itself had any idea where DC Bliss sneaked off to, though many of his colleagues had guessed a girl was involved.

Thinking about that made him reflect more on Hazel's fears. He understood how she had picked up on the change in him, no matter how slight, and his understanding stretched into why she had arrived at the wrong conclusion. She could not possibly know how he was acting while he was at work, but outside of the job he had allowed his manner to alter, possibly going as far as to make it obvious that he was holding something back. Bliss still thought his old man had an inkling, but he regretted putting doubt in Hazel's mind.

On the positive side, he had one more day to make it through after this one. And by the second day of his thirtieth year on planet Earth, he would have an undercover win to his name, a long career as a detective ahead of him, and a life with the most gorgeous creature in the world to look forward to. All that and a Martin acoustic to practice with. Everything was good in Jimmy Bliss's life, and he wasn't ever going to screw that up.

SEVENTEEN

I N THE LEAD UP to the Friday night sting, Bliss was on a run of short shifts. He had to spend some time at his flat in case he was being observed. He also visited a few local shops, pubs and cafes. He was enjoying the Cosworth more than he ought to – he loved to drive, and enjoyed the rush of speed. The car was capable of taking him well above the limit, which was why he restricted his drives to sensible roads and not the motorways. It was hard to resist that kind of temptation, especially as, when he wasn't at home and not on duty, he had to act like Vincent Styles as often as possible.

He arrived at the station in time for a mid-morning briefing. There would be another one the following day, but over the past week it had become policy to discuss the operation in every detail on a daily basis.

The occasional wrinkle appeared, and was subsequently ironed out. No strategy was foolproof, but at all times the team weighed the O'Shea plan against police countermeasures. Bliss was seeing what it meant to take part in a huge set-up, and he expected it to be the first of many. Most of all, he hoped he would get to lead the majority of them in the future.

Shortly after lunch, Fleet beckoned him and Mitchell into the side room they had squirrelled themselves away in previously. Beaming, and clearly pleased with his efforts, the PC laid out what he had for them. 'Our woman *is* Angie Lawson. She is also Angie Borthwick. The latter is her married name.'

'That's interesting,' Mitchell said. 'I was expecting the husband to be a lie.'

'In some ways he is. Mr Borthwick is deceased.'

'How did you find that out?' Bliss asked, curiosity getting the better of him.

'Purely by chance. There is a change of name application on file. The reason given is the death of Angie's spouse. But then for reasons known only to Angie, I suspect, she withdrew the application. And yes, before you ask… I do have her address.'

An hour later, Bliss and Mitchell used one of the keys found in Angie's shoulder bag to obtain access to a ground-floor flat on a smart estate close to Roman Road. On the way there, he'd admitted his fear of finding the missing boy lying dead inside the house, the foul odour of putrefaction guiding the way. The sense of relief he felt when he stepped inside the flat to the smell of fresh air was close to overwhelming.

Angie Borthwick's entire life did not take long to pick apart. There were plenty of documents for them to dig around in, but the photo albums told a tale all of their own. Both in what they portrayed and in what they did not. A young Angie Lawson holding a baby to her chest, taken as the proud mother pecked her child on the head. Two full albums' worth of Angie, her boy Michael, her parents and younger sister. Each photograph carefully notated and catalogued. Dozens of snapshots taking the two detectives through Michael's life from a day old right through to the age of five. The last one was dated May 1969.

In a binder, Bliss discovered cuttings from a newspaper: the *East London Advertiser*. There were a couple of dozen in all, filed in chronological order. He read through the first few, nodding and shaking his head in silence. When he was done he puffed out his lips.

'Listen to this,' he said, catching Mitchell's attention. 'When her son was five, Angie took him to the park as she had done on hundreds of previous occasions. On this particular spring day, however, Michael slipped away unseen as his mother bought them both an ice-cream cone. Frantic, she enlisted the help of other people to help search the park and the lake closest to the pavilion café we were just in. The boy had been missing for only five minutes when he was found lying beneath a tree. According to the main article, in one hand he was still clutching a small branch that had apparently snapped off the old oak he'd tried to climb. It seems that as Michael fell, his head struck a more sturdy bough at an awkward angle, snapping the poor little sod's neck.'

Mitchell closed her eyes as if to ward off the image. Bliss handed her the articles and dug into the remaining clippings, which went on to describe the inquest and subsequent funeral, paying close attention to the boy's mother. She had given birth to Michael when just nineteen, the boy's father undisclosed on the birth certificate and seemingly uninvolved with his life at any point. Supportive parents rallied around their daughter, though Angie's sister had made one or two comments about Michael never having a chance with a mother whose negligence had come close to killing the boy on two previous occasions. These statements were never corroborated, and were later retracted.

Bliss felt heat spread across his chest as he read the newspaper columns. Retraction or not, the damage was already done to the grieving mother's reputation. Some people turned against Angie Lawson while she continued to mourn, but as time wore on the newspaper shifted their attentions elsewhere and both Angie and her son were soon forgotten.

Clearly not by his mother, Bliss thought.

He stayed on beyond his shift hours, although he booked himself off duty. He wasn't interested in over-time. Thought of Angie and what had taken place earlier in the week consumed him. Together, he and DC Mitchell – with some additional help from PC Fleet – gradually put the pieces of the puzzle together.

At one point, Mitchell put back her head and sighed. 'It's all so terribly sad. The death of her son turned Angie's previously happy and contented life upside down. From there she followed the wrong path towards the kind of oblivion only offered by alcohol and drugs. She became so lost in the darkness that it also cost her the love of her mother and father who, having endured enough misery and seeing no way back to the daughter they had known and loved, left the area. From what I can tell, they never returned.'

Bliss was nodding, choking up as he revealed what he had discovered. 'During what seems like a relatively stable period for her, Angie met and married Kevin Borthwick, a Geordie lorry driver. A letter he wrote suggests that conquering his own demons led her husband to regard himself as her saviour. He failed, and following a particularly ugly period during which

Angie's drug-induced neurosis bloated into full-blown paranoid schizophrenia, he walked out on her.'

'When the going gets tough, eh? Angie remained in the flat and kept his name, although her own identity appeared to fluctuate depending on the circumstances she found herself in. Her absent husband passed away shortly afterwards.'

'Like you said… terribly sad.'

While Mitchell and Fleet continued to plough through the woman's past, Bliss called the hospital and spoke with Mr Yarwood. The man proved to be a good listener, and he barely interrupted at all as Bliss outlined the progress made so far. The consultant gave the matter some thought before responding.

'In adding what you have discovered to my own close observation and one-to-one discussions with Angela, I feel secure in drawing several conclusions. For the most part, she is able to operate at a level at which she knows who she is, where she is, and what she is doing, in addition to where she has been and what she has done. On other occasions, however, it appears that something will suddenly cause the entire world and her participation in it to shift. It becomes completely unbalanced. Almost alien. More often than not it takes a moment of extreme familiarity as opposed to trauma to incite this dramatic change; a walk in the park, suddenly becoming aware of Michael's pushchair, perhaps even the sight of one of his toys.'

'Is that what happened this time?' Bliss asked.

'I believe so, yes. Precisely that, in fact. According to Angela, Michael's favourite toy was Baloo bear – a character from the film, *The Jungle Book*. She recalled spotting the old toy while pottering about in his bedroom. She picked it up and cuddled it for a while, and that seems to have been the trigger. She remembered nothing else that happened afterwards until finding herself in the psychiatric ward. This was, in my opinion, a culmination of a number of minor psychotic events she had been experiencing over a period of many years.'

'Why toddler?' Bliss asked, curious about this aspect of the woman's breakdown. 'Why did Angie initially refer to him as a toddler?'

Yarwood's reply was immediate. 'I believe Angela came close to losing Michael once before, in the same park, but on that occasion she thought he had gone into the lake. He was about two or three at that point. Angie's mind right now cannot differentiate between any of the times she visited that park. When she thinks of her son she can see him at any age up to the point at which he died. That's why her story is seldom the same when she repeats it.'

Bliss shook his head, a desperate sense of melancholy creeping over him. 'She blames herself for his death.

And on Monday she genuinely believed he was with her and that she had lost him there that very morning.'

'Tragically, that's what her mind is telling her. She is bereft, believing her son is dead, that she is responsible, but also that it happened just a few days ago.'

After thanking Yarwood, Bliss related the salient aspects of his conversation to Mitchell and Fleet. Both appeared to take the news as badly as he had. They discussed it further, but to Bliss it felt as if they were merely raking over the ashes. He left Faith Mitchell to close out the investigation. That's it, he thought. Job done. Nothing to see here. The problem was, he thought it would be a long time before he stopped seeing the horrifying anguish written across the face of a mother who fears she has lost her child.

Later that same night, having spent the rest of the day in a sullen and contemplative mood, he realised further how unlike his father he was in that regard. Despite growing up in a house in which Dennis Bliss left the job at the front door, and even accounting for the old man's stern counsel about taking it to heart, Jimmy realised he had already become a different person entirely.

He met Hazel for a quick drink that evening, but when she asked him to explain his low mood he found himself lost for words. Angie's distress and terror remained squarely in his mind's eye, yet he was unable to describe it in mere words. You had to have been there to fully comprehend, he thought, because it had come off her in waves. And if he could not project what he had seen and felt, how was it possible to make Hazel understand? He wasn't even sure he did, not entirely.

Reassuring his girlfriend that all would be well come the weekend, he hugged her close. He thought he might find it hard to let go, knowing what was happening the following day. But instead his mind was on Angie and Michael, and in clinging to Hazel the way he did, Bliss knew it was because he never wanted to experience such an all-encompassing loss.

EIGHTEEN

BLISS FELT ON EDGE as Friday slipped towards the evening. He maintained a composed exterior, behaving as if taking part in a heist was just another job to him. But anxiety gnawed away at his insides, and to ward it off he kept himself busy. There was something playing on his mind, and eventually restlessness won the day. He had time to put the matter behind him, and at the very least it would keep him occupied for a couple of hours.

He first visited another unit located on the ground floor of the building he was stationed in, where he chatted with two fellow detectives. Bliss then collected his car and drove out to Whitechapel. He pulled to the kerb on a dead end road off Stepney Way, where he sat for a while observing the car park opposite. Every so often a vehicle slowed as it neared the structure's exit, at which point a handful of women stepped out of the shadows to put themselves on display. Many of the vehicles simply pulled away again, often faster than they had arrived. But one eventually came to a halt, and moments later one of the women slipped into the vehicle alongside the driver. Bliss looked on as they spoke, before the two drove off together. Brake lights flickered briefly before the vehicle turned towards the car park entrance.

Elaine must have been with a punter when he arrived, as he noticed her join the other prostitutes when a small red van pulled over. Bliss dug the palm of his hand into the centre of his steering wheel and pressed down three times in quick succession. The sound of the horn alerted the women, and their heads popped up like startled meerkats. All but one scowled in his direction before scattering like ants beneath a downpour of boiling water. The red van sped off down the street and took the next available turning on two wheels. Elaine clocked who was in the car, waved at Bliss and tottered across the road on four-inch heels. She pulled open the passenger door and slipped in beside him.

'Was that absolutely necessary?' she asked. 'You scared them all away.'

'Good. I'm hoping I can do the same with you.'

'Oh, don't start that again, Jimmy.'

'No, it's different this time. Seriously.'

'How d'you mean?'

'You helped me out the other night. I want to repay the favour. In the past I've tried persuading you to give up walking the streets, but in truth it's been a pretty feeble effort on my part. I was thinking about you earlier, and it didn't sit right with me knowing you were still out here. Doing what you do.'

Elaine groaned and shook her head. 'If you're going to try talking me out of it again, save your breath. When my body gives up on me, I'll give up on it. Until then, this is the way I earn a living. It's either this or half a dozen kids and living off benefits on some poxy sink estate, Jimmy. That ain't me, and you should know it by now.'

'That's not what this is about. I've broached the subject of you working for an escort agency a couple of times before. On this occasion I've come better prepared to back up my own argument.' Seeing Elaine start to bristle with indignation, Bliss held up a hand to pacify her. 'Hear me out. If I can't convince you this time, I'll drop it and never mention it again. Deal?'

She pushed out a long, deep breath. He read her eyes. Saw the scepticism and understood it. But he pushed on anyway. 'Deal?' he prompted again.

'All right. Deal. Say what you have to say, Jimmy. I'm losing money sat on my arse here.'

Bliss swallowed. At least he'd got her to listen. Now for the hard part. 'Today I had a chat with a couple of people from Vice. I mentioned your name. They knew who you were and that you're a good snout for me. That's one of the reasons you've not been pulled in for a while. I asked them about escort agencies. Most of them – as you rightly told me last time I brought them up – are virtually as bad as working the streets. But they did mention a couple that see themselves as a step up from the rest. They keep their girls in decent flats, make sure they're well looked after, protected, healthy, and although none of it is above board, it removes their girls from a great deal of risk. One of the Vice detectives told me that if you wanted in, they'd have a word. Favours could be exchanged and the agency would make room for you.'

Bliss was expecting an immediate reaction, but Elaine said nothing for a good while. She stared out through the windscreen, though he thought she was probably taking a long, hard look at herself and the life she had chosen to live.

'Don't they want only younger girls?' she finally said, still peering straight ahead. 'Even if they took me in now, what happens to me in a year or so?'

'These people make a decent bunce out of running mature women, too. Provided you keep yourself in decent nick and healthy – which to them means no drugs and not too much booze – you can keep the punters coming in for a good while yet. Longer than you can out here, I reckon. Look, Elaine, I know you prefer to operate freely, but sooner or later you're going to either have to work for a pimp or suffer the consequences if you keep saying no. I don't want to see you get carved up next time you refuse. Let me do this favour for you.'

She seemed to consider his plea, but then said, 'What about the information I feed you? That's bound to dry up if I'm not out here on the streets.'

He shook his head. 'Not completely. You get around. People open up to you. And even if that side of it stops, it's worth it to me. I want to know you're as safe as you can be. You won't lose out on it, I promise you. You'll earn more, so you won't need the few quid I bung you.'

'I don't know, Jimmy. It's tempting, and you're sweet to think of me.' She nodded across the street, towards the car park and her fellow prostitutes tentatively making their way back. 'But maybe this is where I belong.'

'Not from where I'm sitting you don't. Look, what have you got to lose? Give it a couple of months, three maybe. See how it works out. The streets will always be out here waiting for you if you decide you can't live without them. But I think you can. In an ideal world you know I'd have you off the game altogether. But if this is the best I can do for you, Elaine, please just have a crack at it.'

Bliss read her eyes again, and this time he saw hope. For both of them. He winked at her. 'Good girl. You know it makes sense. You at the same address?'

'Where else?'

'Terrific. I'll sort out the details and drop round your place on Monday. Tuesday at the latest. How does that sound?'

'To be honest… a bit scary. But then this shit scares me at least half a dozen times a day.'

Bliss patted her on the leg. 'So let's hope we can address that at the same time,' he said. 'You're doing the right thing. I'm proud of you.'

NINETEEN

THEY WERE COMING OFF the brow of a hill and bearing down on the industrial shopping estate when John spoke from his position in the back of the van. 'Drive on past the junction, Georgie boy. Take the next one instead.'

Jimmy Bliss heard something in the man's tone to give him pause. In the early hours of the morning, he and Ringo had picked up the getaway vehicles and driven over to Woodford to leave them in place for when they dumped the van. Ringo had seemed his breezy self; if he knew anything about the ransacking of the flat he didn't let on. Meeting up with John again had concerned Bliss, but he was as certain as he could be that if he'd been rumbled, he would have known about it long before the pre-job gathering. Men like the O'Sheas did nothing by half. They doled out swift justice.

As it turned out, John had been buzzing from the word go, pumping them up with a lot of fist-shaking and back-slapping as the four men changed clothes and climbed aboard the van. With Bliss holding the back door open, John had paused, one foot hooked up on the lip. 'You all right there, Georgie boy?' he asked, his voice in sing-song mode. His lips twisted, but his dead eyes were unfathomable.

Bliss nodded. 'Yeah. Of course.'

'You sure about that? You look a wee bit nervous to me.'

'That's because I *am* nervous. Believe me, John, it's how you want me to be. I'm at my best when I'm jumpy.'

'So, no problems?'

Bliss paused, slipping back into Vincent Styles's head. He met John's tight gaze. 'As it happens, I'm a bit pissed off. My gaff was broken into Tuesday night.'

'Is that right? They get away with much?'

'Bugger all to get away *with*. Still, I'd like to have caught the little bastards at it. They turned the place over. It was a right two-and-eight by the time I walked in.'

'Sounds rough. Maybe that's something you ought to have mentioned before now.'

Shrugging, Bliss said, 'Didn't seem worth wasting valuable air on it. I had a mess to clear up. No big deal.'

'And what if it was the filth?'

'Nah, they'd've been more thorough. This was an amateur job bungled by a couple of scrotes. Kids, most likely. Old Bill would've torn the place up, floorboards and all.'

John had given him one final hard look before nodding. He'd been relatively silent since, which was understandable given the circumstances. But Bliss had no idea where this new instruction was coming from, and he immediately wondered if the two were connected. 'The second junction? The one we're supposed to use coming back out of the estate?'

'That's the one.'

'But why? Makes no sense.'

'Don't fret about it, Georgie boy. Change of plan, is all. As it goes, a change of plan only where you're concerned. The rest of us knew the real plan all along.'

Bliss drove on, his mind spinning. Had they tumbled to him after all? He reacted appropriately. 'You're telling me this now? What the fuck?'

'Ah, don't get all lairy and bent out of shape. The truth is, I've known Paul and Ringo for a while now. I like them and trust them both like I do my own brother. You I don't know, Georgie boy. So, I don't have the same level of trust where you're concerned.'

Switching on the anger as he imagined Vincent Styles would, Bliss snapped. 'What the fuck is going on here!? Did you think if I knew the truth I might try and do the job on my own or something? What don't you trust about me, John?'

'Why does it matter? Just do what I tell you and you'll be taken care of when we divvy up. You'll still get your cut.'

Bliss knew he ought to bail out, hoping his colleagues were monitoring him closely enough to adapt swiftly when they saw things go the wrong way. But Vincent Styles wouldn't behave that way. He'd push it. Which was what Bliss did next.

'Fuck my cut!' he roared. 'I'll stand my reputation alongside yours any day of the week. Any of you. I've never been caught and I've never had to deal with the filth, and now you have the fucking neck to question my loyalty?'

'Yeah, I do have the neck,' John shot back. 'And you'd better wind yours in, Georgie boy, if you know what's good for you. Remember who you're talking to here.'

Silence filled the inside of the van with tension for a minute or so. Bliss hit the indicator and pulled off at the second junction as instructed. 'So where *are* we going?'

'Just follow the directions I give you. Your job is the same as it was before, we work it exactly as we planned. It's just a different location.'

Thinking it all through, Bliss checked off the roles they were each playing. Ringo, who sat alongside him in the passenger seat, had pulled a Motorola MicroTac mobile phone out of the glove compartment to call in the cancellation of the shout his planted incendiary device would have caused. Bliss had never known the relevant store codes nor the destination of the call the fireman had to contact, but in less than thirty seconds Ringo's face was wreathed in smiles.

'We're a go,' he'd said. 'They're being turned back.'

Until now, everything seemed to have gone off like clockwork. But Bliss felt a knot tighten in his stomach as he realised the awful truth about this change of plan.

'Fuck!' he said, thumping the steering wheel with the side of his fist.

'Oi, settle down,' Paul told him. He said it aggressively, but did not raise his voice.

'I wish you'd told me, is all. I've been practicing for that bloody safe for weeks now. Do you have any idea what kind they have in this other place we're hitting? Supposing it's something I've never come across before?'

'You're a bloody safecracker,' John said. Bliss could feel the man's breath on the back of his neck, and it made his flesh crawl. 'Just do your fucking job. And there's no need to go getting your knickers in a twist – it's the same safe.'

'Same level of security?'

'Of course. We're not stupid, George. It's the exact same safe I've been telling you about all along. I lied about where it was, that's all.'

That's as maybe, Bliss thought, feeling a trickle of sweat running down from his hairline. *But it's not the one I have the combination for.*

'Did you also make sure it has a mechanical lock and not an electronic one? It has to be a rotary dial, John, not some push button pad.'

'What's the difference?' Paul asked. 'A safe is a safe, right?'

Bliss had been reading up on safe types and locks in case he was grilled by his fellow Beatles. He shook his head in exasperation. 'There's a world of difference. With a mechanical dial lock, they basically all function the same way. The ones on this particular safe do, because they use the same wheel pack. You have four complete revolutions of the dial left when finding the first number, three right for the second, two left for number three, and finally another right for combination number four. Essentially, you're priming the lock first, and then you feel and listen for the right one to start opening up. Once you've picked up your wheels you wait for the fence lever to drop.'

'Is that why some Petermen use one of those doctor's stethoscopes?'

'Precisely. But an electronic number pad works in a completely different way, disengaging the lock with power as opposed to feel. If this safe has one of those, then we're screwed.'

Bliss hoped this might convince John to call the job off until he could be certain about the lock type, but the man sitting up close behind him was chuckling to himself. 'Don't lose your bottle now, George, there's a good lad. And don't fret yourself about the fecking lock. You have your mechanical dial as promised. This is not our first time out of nappies.'

His thoughts frazzled by no longer having the code, Bliss followed directions as John gave them, eventually pulling up behind a range of stores that all looked the same size and shape. About a dozen people stood outside, all gathered together in an area on the opposite side of the road from where John told him to stop the van. When they came to a halt, Ringo jumped out and jogged across the road, calling out for the manager to make himself known. Bliss heard him tell the man they would need twenty or so minutes while they checked out what they thought was more than likely a false alarm, and would also need to reset the system. The manager handed over a bunch of keys. When Ringo climbed back into the van, he pointed ahead and to the right. He advised Bliss that if he swung around there, he could then back all the way in to the loading ramp over to the left. There they would be tucked away out of view from anybody who happened to pass by.

Bliss nodded in silence. It was a fine plan. The thorn in their side now was him, because he had no clue how to crack the safe open. Fear settled over him like a sheen of ice. He had a good idea how John would react if the safe was not opened, and for a moment his thoughts drifted to Hazel. For her sake as well as his own, he had to remain calm and think his way out the mess he found himself in.

Once inside the building, both Ringo and Paul went to work resetting the alarm and door systems. John reminded them to then ransack the banks of locked cabinet drawers. Bliss carried the empty holdalls, while John dragged along a box of tools on wheels in case there were any bolts or chains in need of breaking through, or drawers to bust open. The pair walked along a short corridor and stopped to wait. Less than thirty seconds later, a set of double doors in front of them popped open. The two men walked through into a larger area with plain breeze-block walls and turned right to head down toward the offices.

'What is this place?' Bliss asked. He knew it was no warehouse full of electronic goods. The building's footprint was significantly smaller.

'Wholesale jewellers,' John told him. 'A blinding haul at any time, but today they also have a new shipment of uncut diamonds in the safe. We'll bust open some trays and drawers to clear them out, too, but those diamonds are what we're mainly here for.'

Bliss was immediately alert to what John had said. 'Bust open trays and drawers? But the staff will notice the damage as soon as they come back inside.'

'You'd better put your foot down when we leave then, hadn't you, George? That is the other reason you're here, right?'

'You told us we'd have all the time we needed. That the staff might not be aware of anything being wrong until they next opened the safe.'

John flashed a grin. 'I thought you'd cottoned on by now, Georgie boy. Sometimes I tell porkies.'

Shaking his head, Bliss wondered how the evening could possibly get worse. He had no idea what he was going to do now with a safe whose combination he did not have. He had a vague notion of how they worked, but had no feel or sensitivity when it came to using a dial and listening to the whispering levers as they shifted. Right now he was starting to think that his best hope was if his team had sussed out what was happening and were already surrounding the place.

John stepped ahead and threw open the office door. At the back of the tiny room stood two safes. There was just one problem.

'Fuck it!' Bliss said. Between them and the safe were wall-to-wall steel bars. A barred door was closed, and he had already spotted the electronic lock. 'I hope you've got the combination for that, John.'

The man winked at him and took a couple of steps forward. He put a hand on the door and gave it a shove. It swung open silently. He turned and grinned. 'Electronic locks and alarms are a thing of beauty, Georgie boy. It's almost too easy.'

Bliss blew out a puff of air. He stepped beyond his partner in crime and studied the two safes. The one on the right was the make and model Bliss had expected to find. But as they moved closer to it, he suddenly stopped in his tracks.

'What's the matter?' John asked him. 'It has the right kind of lock, yeah? You were expecting a dial, you got a dial.'

Bliss nodded with his mouth hanging open, the relief currently flooding his veins making him feel a little lightheaded. His hopes had been answered. He turned to face his accomplice. 'Yeah. It has a dial just like you said. But the problem is, John, it also has a key lock. I can handle the combination like I always said I could. The problem is, without a key as well, we're completely screwed.'

TWENTY

THE ONE THING BLISS didn't expect was for the big Irishman to panic. He looked on in alarm as John kicked out in a state of frenzy at the rolling tool box, and then did the same to an office chair, swearing fiercely as he did so. His large face became inflamed with rage, and Bliss started to wonder when it might turn on him.

'You're a safecracker!' John cried, his eyes narrowing to the thinnest of slits. 'It's still a fucking safe. Open the bastard thing.'

'It's not that I can't open it,' Bliss said softly, gathering his wits. 'It's time we're talking about. These locks are among the best in the world. Even if I had the right tools – which I don't, because nobody mentioned a sodding key to me – it could take me thirty or forty minutes just to pick the lock.'

'So we drill it.'

'No. Not a key lock for a safe you don't. This isn't someone's front door, John.'

'There has to be a way.'

'There is. We need the key. Each lock comes with two keys, so I'm guessing the manager has one and there's another hidden away somewhere.'

'You're telling me you need a fucking key?! What bloody use are you to me? I thought you were some big deal.' The hulking man was sweating now, his face still fiery, veins as prominent as knotted rope.

Bliss stood his ground, thoughts ticking over all the while. 'John, you have to calm yourself down and listen to reason. Unless you're doing a job overnight and the cracker has all the time to ply his trade properly, you can't expect anybody to walk in here unprepared and tackle both locks in the time we have. If I'd known beforehand, I would have said all this and we could have come up with a different plan. But right now, as things stand, you're asking for the impossible.'

'Fuck it!' John snarled. Then he turned and headed for the doorway.

'Where are you going?' Bliss asked, hoping the job was about to be called off.

John stopped and turned, his features still creased with rage. 'If the key is what we need, then we get the key. I'll go back out there and talk the manager into coming inside with me, tell him we have a problem we'd like him to have a look at.'

Bliss shook his head. 'No, no. Don't do that. You're not thinking clearly. He saw me and Ringo driving in. How do you think he's going to react when you bowl up outside?'

The man's entire heavy frame slumped as if punctured. His chin came down, and Bliss could see his tongue protruding through clamped teeth as this fresh information seeped in.

'I'll go,' Bliss said. He wanted to take matters further, to see the operation out, but he was not willing to put an innocent civilian at risk under any circumstances. It wasn't a perfect end to the op by any means, but once outside he could call in his team and sweep up the remaining three Beatles. Not the Mr Big he wanted, and not in the conditions he would have preferred, but being back to their original score wasn't so awful. They wouldn't have the stolen cash they'd expected as firm evidence, but the crew were not going to talk their way out of this mess.

'No, you're all right,' came a voice from the doorway as Bliss started to leave. It was Ringo, who had probably overheard everything. 'I was wondering what was going on. I take it our Peterman fucked up at the first hurdle?'

'You watch your fucking mouth,' Bliss snapped, squaring up to the young fireman. 'I fucked nothing up. You want to blame someone, blame whoever suggested leaving me clueless until we were almost here. Our problem is this safe has two locks and one of them requires a key. No way we can get in and out of here now with the diamonds if we don't have either that key or the time for me to bypass it.'

Ringo warded him off with a raised hand. 'All right, calm the fuck down. I'll get him in here.'

Bliss's mind worked furiously. Once the manager was inside with them, everything became more difficult to manage. It also made their escape all the more awkward, and he couldn't see that ending well for the man who ran this place.

'What have you got against me going?' he asked, walking slowly towards the corridor outside the office. 'I'm getting a bit sick and tired of not being trusted. I can talk the bloke into coming back inside with me just as easily as you, Ringo. So why you and not me? Maybe you're the one we should be looking sideways at.'

Ringo's face creased into sharp angles and he made a move towards Bliss, both hands now clenched. But as things looked to have turned nasty, John stood between them and he turned to fill the doorway with his bulk. 'You two stop squabbling like a couple of old biddies. You're wasting time. Time we don't have to spare. It's my fault there's a lack of trust, and I hold my hands up to that. But it stops here. We need to keep our wits about us and carry on. George, back the fuck up. Ringo… go get our man in here. Now!'

Without another word, Ringo disappeared along the corridor. Bliss sighed and walked back over to the safe. He stood there looking at it, arms folded, shaking his head. 'If I had longer, I'd crack this bastard.' He said it as if to himself, but wanting to be overheard.

'You want to have a go at the combination lock while we're waiting?' John said, coming up behind him. He seemed calmer now, which had been Bliss's intention.

'No. That's not a good idea. Fact is, the safe could be rigged. Some people set them up so that if you do them in the wrong order, it triggers an alarm.'

'Paul handled the alarms, so you're fine.'

'It could have a separate local feed. Depends on how tricky these bastards have been.'

This time John nodded as if he understood how such things worked. He couldn't know Bliss was making it up as he went along. It sounded logical, so he'd gone with his gut. Paul showed up a moment later, and John explained the delay. Bliss felt the newcomer's eyes drift across to him, and he deliberately challenged the man's gaze.

'You two had best get yourselves out of the way,' Bliss said. 'Better not to let the manager see either of you before he finds out what's going on. We don't want to freak him out too soon.'

'Fuck that,' John said. 'I'm going nowhere.'

Beside him, Paul shook his head. 'Me neither.'

The three of them stood inside the office in complete silence. Bliss's brain worked harder at this problem than any other he'd encountered before, but for the time being he was coming up without any answers. His main fear was what John might do to the manager to keep him quiet as they made their getaway. They all looked up as footsteps echoed along the passage, two voices low and unexcited. Ringo had done the trick, it seemed.

That was until the manager was confronted by three other men rather than the one he'd expected. He looked between them and knew immediately what was going on. Bliss realised it would draw attention his way, but he decided he had to act and get between the manager and the others. He grabbed hold of the man by the lapels of his suit jacket and aggressively bundled him across the room, through the opening in the steel bars, until they were both facing the floor-standing safe.

'Listen up,' he said, 'because I'm only going to say this one time. We hoped to crack the combination while you were still outside waiting for the all clear. But we weren't expecting the key lock as well. I'm sure by now you realise what's what, so I'm telling you nicely: open the safe and do so without triggering an alarm. Unlock it in the correct order, and when you spin that dial I'd better be seeing it turn left first.'

The manager who, according to the nameplate on the door to the office, was called Coker, stood over six foot, but for a fairly well-built man he looked soft. His physique had never counted for a lot, as far as Bliss could tell. He wore a pale grey suit which seemed to match his current pallor. Maybe mid-fifties, his hair had all but vanished from the gleaming dome of his head, with ridiculous clown-like bushes of grey tufted around both ears. Bliss expected the man to swallow back his fear and cooperate fully.

Instead, Coker wet his lips and said without inflection, 'And what if I refuse?'

At which point, John snapped the lock on the rolling tool box and pulled out a shotgun with sections of both ends sawn off. He held it up at around waist height, the twin barrels aiming at a slight upward angle. 'This is what happens if you refuse,' he said, a thin smile touching his lips.

To Bliss's complete shock, the manager didn't fold. Instead he matched the grim smile and said, 'You use that on me and you'll never get inside that safe. I'm the only one who knows where the key is.'

Stalemate.

Except that John wasn't used to things not going his way. He sniffed once and set his stance. 'In that case, we'll make do with stripping out everything you have tucked away inside your cabinets,' he growled at Coker. 'Which makes you, old son, entirely superfluous.'

And with that, he hoisted the weapon.

TWENTY-ONE

Bliss didn't know what came over him, but as he saw the weapon come up, he threw himself forward to put himself directly between the two men. Now the shotgun was pointing at his own chest, and the thought of what might happen next caused his legs to weaken and tremble.

'Hold on, hold on,' he said, hands raised. His tongue snaked out to moisten his lips. 'Take it easy, John. Walk it back. There's no need for this to turn uglier still. Let me sort it for you.'

But the big man was shaking his head, dark anger written across his face. 'Get out of the way, George, or so help me I'll take you out along with this bastard.'

'For fuck's sake, John, give me one crack at him. You want those uncut diamonds, don't you?'

'You think you can do what me and this can't?' He indicated the sawn-off.

Without waiting for a response, Bliss spun and leaned in towards the man whose eyes revealed the horror he felt deep inside. 'Mate, as brave as you are I know you're shitting yourself right now. You must also know that if my pal here pulls both triggers your world will end before you're even aware of it. I don't know if you're bluffing or not. To be honest, I'm not too sure about my pal, either. But the thing is, mate, I never do. So, you'd better listen to me. Your best option right now is to do exactly as I say. You ready?'

The man nodded, tried to answer, but found no words.

'First up, you *are* going to open that safe. Then, we're going to take what we came for, after which me and my mates are going to walk out of here. Once we're outside, we're going to jump back into the van and drive away. You'll give us a fifteen minute head start and then you'll call your staff back inside the building. Understand?'

'I won't do it,' Coker said, lifting his chin as he found his voice once again.

'Yeah, you will. And the reason you're going to do it is because of your family. I clocked the ring on your finger, the photos on your desk. You have a wife and two children, possibly grandchildren. So here's everything you need to know: you are going to open up that safe and let us do our thing, and when you tell your story afterwards you only saw me and my passenger. You don't open up, you fuck us about, I'll find out where you live and I'll torture your wife and anyone else I find inside the house with her at the time. Then I'll find out where your children live and do the same with them. If you let us do what we came here to do, but later mention anyone else being involved when you talk to old Bill after it's all over, one day soon I'll send a crew of men to pay you and your family a visit. They will make sure you watch every single family member die a slow, agonising death, and only then will they take time with you. I do hope you understand me, because I did warn you I'm saying it just the one time.'

Coker was silently weeping now. Tears spilled from both eyes; his mouth hung open, but for some reason he made no sound. It was the kind of silence only utter terror can convey. Bliss felt sickened by the images he had put inside the innocent man's head. But rather a series of terrifying thoughts than gaping holes in his face or chest.

'You can point that thing elsewhere,' Bliss said, looking back over his shoulder at John. His gaze dropped to the gun. 'He'll do as he's told and not say a word about it.'

The big Dubliner pursed his lips and nodded. 'Impressive. Put a chill up my spine, I don't mind admitting.'

'You can add that to my list of charms. No charge.'

John turned his eyes towards the manager. 'Time is not on your side, pal. Make a decision. Your man here bought you a few seconds, but I am not a patient armed blagger.' As if he needed to emphasise the point, he pulled the shotgun into firing position once again.

It did not take Coker long to make up his mind. Moments later, while Paul and Ringo cleaned out the safe, Bliss surreptitiously eyed their gang's leader. He was twitchy, and with his finger virtually caressing the trigger, the possibility of an accidental discharge was high. Bliss had to think fast and act quickly.

'John,' he said, reaching for the man's attention. When he turned his head, Bliss indicated with his own that the gang leader should step in closer. Keeping his voice low, he continued. 'You're not going to do anything rash, are you?'

'What d'you mean by that?'

'I mean, I'm hoping you came tooled up to apply a threat only if absolutely necessary and not because you want to use it.'

'That depends on him.'

'He opened the safe. That's all we need from him.'

'Other than his silence afterwards.'

That same terrible truth had crossed Bliss's mind, which is why he'd exaggerated the threat when talking to Coker. The manager was supposed to see two faces

– his and Ringo's. Neither were known by sight to the police. But now Coker could describe all four men, and Declan O'Shea was a known face. Matching a description to the type of job that had been pulled off would be a piece of cake for whoever investigated.

Bliss knew exactly who would be carrying out that investigation. But John didn't. With things having gone so badly wrong, the big man had to have realised he was vulnerable. Which meant the manager had to go. Somehow, Bliss needed to prevent that from happening.

'Silence, yeah,' he said. 'But not permanently, eh? I've been thinking about how we can handle it differently. We can lock him up in here with the safes. Then we tell his staff when we drive away that he is resetting everything and he'll be out to let them know when they can all return indoors. That'll give us the time we need to get away. The man is broken, John. My threat got him to open the safe. You think he's going to tell the police about you or Paul after what I said to him? He may or may not have been willing to risk his own neck, but he won't let anything happen to his wife or kids.'

John's brow furrowed. 'What's your concern? Why are you bothered about him?'

'I'm not. I couldn't give a toss about him. I'm bothered about me. Old Bill coming after me for a blagging is one thing. Murder's a different matter altogether. All

I'm saying is… keep your cool, yeah? We have this. Let's just go without spilling any blood.'

The big man nodded indifferently, but Bliss thought he would see sense. Provided Coker didn't say or do anything stupid. Bliss started to relax, his guts having been twisted ever since he saw the key lock in the safe. Looking at the long game, he knew his plan was still in play assuming they managed to get away from this place precisely as planned.

'Got it all,' Paul said at that moment, zipping shut the holdall he'd been stuffing items into.

'Me, too,' Ringo chimed in, his wide easy grin back in place. He was enjoying himself.

John gave a thumbs-up. 'Get yourselves in the van.' He turned to Bliss. 'You, too. I'll secure your man here and join you in a minute or two at most.'

Bliss stared up into his eyes. They were dull and gave nothing away of his inner thoughts. 'Please, John. Trust me. This man will never tell. Not as long as his family are alive. Do the right thing here, yeah.'

O'Shea raised a hand. As Bliss flinched, the big man patted him on the cheek. 'Calm down, Georgie boy. You asked me to trust you. Now it's time for you to trust me.'

TWENTY-TWO

THEIR EXIT WAS EXEMPLARY. On the way out, Jimmy put a foot on the brake while Ringo told the staff still grouped outside that Mr Coker would be with them as soon as the entire system had been reset. Less than a minute later they stopped off in an alleyway between two lines of warehouses, where he and the fireman peeled off the livery and tossed it all into an industrial-sized rubbish receptacle. The magnetic number plates went the same way. Bliss then took them out of the estate and back onto the road heading east. He kept within the speed limit at all times.

Outwardly calm, his insides were roiling. He had questioned John with a single look when the crew leader eventually climbed back into the van. The man gave no indication either way as to what he had done, but Bliss felt sure he would have heard the shot if the big man had killed the manager. Not knowing for sure niggled him, though. Coker was a complete innocent, and though this was a sanctioned undercover operation, Bliss couldn't help but feel partially responsible. If he had not stepped up inside the office, the manager might already be dead, which was some consolation. Still it gnawed away at him.

He'd been feeding off adrenaline since John had announced the change of location for the hit. He'd felt the full force of the spotlight thrust upon him, a bit like a fly beneath a powerful magnifying glass. He'd entered Coker's office still unsure of what to do, because clearly there was no way he was going to get the safe open. His one hope at that stage was that the safe would be different, something brand new and untested, which might provide him with an excuse at the very least. Seeing the key slot had come as such an overwhelming relief.

Bliss was still thinking about that moment when John tapped him on the shoulder, almost causing him to cry out. 'You did well back there, Georgie boy. I didn't know if that fucker was going to open up for us or not. What you said to him might've made all the difference.'

'Would you have shot him if he hadn't?'

'Of course.'

He said it so nonchalantly that Bliss felt a tiny piece of his own humanity die. He simply could not fathom why life meant so little to the likes of Declan O'Shea.

He felt as if the Irishman was expecting some kind of response. 'I'm glad he did the right thing, then,' he said. 'I wouldn't have wanted to get his blood and grey matter all over me.'

John laughed and clapped him on the shoulder one last time. Bliss drove on, feeling repulsed. He kept an eye out in the mirrors for his team, wondering how they had reacted when they realised the job location had changed. The plan had been to mount observation on the way in, but not so tight that either Paul or John would have spotted it from the back of the van. His team would watch him enter the estate and follow when he exited, but he had instead entered at the other end of the complex. From their planned observations points, his colleagues could not possibly have seen him drive in or turn off towards the wholesale jewellers.

Bliss silently asked himself what would have happened at that point. As the minutes ticked by and he failed to show, one of his team would surely have thought of putting a call in to the fire service to ask about the aborted shout. That would have given them the new address, and Bliss was confident in his team to think they had made adjustments and were somewhere behind him now. They were good enough for him not to pick them out on the busy road.

Leaving the getaway cars in the car park behind a disused pub had been an inspired choice. The place was derelict because its location was less than prime, on a quiet stretch of road with no houses nearby. It was the kind of pub you had to either drive to or pay for cabs, and patrons eventually decided to take their custom elsewhere.

As they approached the pub, Bliss checked ahead and in his rear-view mirror. With no traffic moving either way, he pulled off the road, the van's heavy tyres crunching over gravel as he nursed it behind the darkened building where it could no longer be seen by anyone passing by. The BMW and Audi stood where he and Ringo had left them.

The plan now was for Ringo to set a timed incendiary device to make sure the van went up in flames in the early hours of the morning. He would join Bliss in the BMW, while John and Paul took off in the Audi. The following day they'd all meet in the snooker hall. On hearing this part of the plan for the first time, Bliss had started to feel uncomfortable. John taking Paul with him told Bliss the two men were closer than either had let on. With Ringo a similarly unknown face to the crew as far as he was aware, Bliss wondered if they would ever see the other two men once the crew separated. But it was Ringo who had voiced the fear first.

'That don't sound right to me,' he'd said. 'How do me and George know you two ain't going to tuck us up?'

A dense black cloud seemed to pass across John's face, which grew instantly rigid. 'People always get one chance with me,' he said calmly. 'That was yours, Ringo. You question me like that again and you're out. Permanently, if you catch my drift. If you don't know my reputation by now, I suggest you ask around. When I do a job with other fellahs, those fellahs get paid and they get looked after. It's the way I do business, because it's the only way *to* do business. Don't be disrespecting me like again. We clear on that, Ringo?'

After a moment, the fireman nodded. Whether he was too scared to speak or had chosen to have the last word by saying nothing, Bliss didn't know. He was glad Ringo had asked the question, though. John's reply had been resounding and also made a lot of sense: when you relied on a gang to pull off armed blaggings and robberies, trust had to work all ways. It was a dangerous business, and there was no room for lingering doubt or suspicion.

Bliss reminded himself of that now as he climbed in behind the wheel of the BMW. John had earlier made it clear that he, Paul and Ringo were closer than had previously been suggested, leaving Bliss to wonder how much of what he'd seen and heard had been staged for his benefit.

Ringo was still leaning into the back of the van, tinkering with the incendiary device. Paul was already sitting in the passenger seat of the Audi, and as John pulled open the driver's side door, he glanced across at Bliss and nodded. It was a gesture of appreciation, giving the man he knew as Vincent Styles his due for a job well done. In all the excitement of a successful heist, it seemed to have been forgotten that the Peterman hadn't actually cracked the safe at all.

Bliss heard the Audi's big two litre engine turn over. And again. And for a third time. He'd already started up the Beemer and it was humming. He swallowed hard, and as Ringo jogged across, Bliss jumped out and dashed over to the Audi. He pulled the driver's door open.

'What's up?' he asked.

'The fecking thing won't start.'

'Try it again.'

John turned the key, his foot on the accelerator.

Again the engine cranked but failed to ignite.

'It might be flooded. Did you pump it first?'

'I don't fucking know!' John roared back at him.

'All right. Calm down. Leave it a couple of minutes and try again. If it's flooded, let it settle before giving it another turnover.'

'I know how to start a fucking car! This is your fault. You stole a fucking lemon.'

'There was nothing wrong with it last night. In fact, I drove this one and as I pulled up alongside Ringo, he mentioned how well-tuned it sounded. Ask him.'

John slapped a hand on the wheel and turned the engine over one more time. Bliss had counted on the man's impatience. The Audi refused to start.

'Stand back!' John snapped at him, throwing the door wide open this time. He turned to Paul, sitting alongside him. 'Come on. Change of plan.'

Bliss had to hide the smile he felt building up inside him. Change of plan for the other three this time, but not for him. His own had worked perfectly. He'd not lied to John about Ringo's comment regarding the car's nicely tuned engine. But even German engineering couldn't defeat the immobiliser he had switched on before leaving it the night before.

TWENTY-THREE

'WHEN WE GET THERE, you stay with the motor,' John told him.

The crew leader had replaced Ringo in the shotgun seat. His mood had soured and his temper was foul. Bliss had an idea it was because whoever they were driving to meet put fear into O'Shea the way O'Shea did into others. He certainly didn't want to lose face by arriving at the man's home with the entire gang in tow. Other than providing directions, the command for them to remain inside the vehicle was the first thing John had said since they'd driven out of the pub car park.

As he drove, Bliss speculated as to where their ultimate destination might be. They passed through Romford and Gallows Corner, moving deeper into Essex. He thought of the list of villains out this way and felt his skin tingling in excitement. When John told him to head into the Hutton Mount area of Brentwood, Bliss knew exactly what kind of money and influence they were dealing with here. No wonder John was nervous.

In truth, Bliss had expected the man to direct him back into London and the east end. For a week or so now, he'd had it in mind that the O'Shea brothers were working for the Doyle family. Fellow Dubliners, the Doyles ran Islington and Clerkenwell, their reach filtering into other areas such as Hoxton and Whitechapel, and they had seemed the most likely fit for Declan and Dermot. Now he wondered if the figure leading John around by the nose was somebody known to the police at all, given the major players mostly kept themselves at such a distance their names never came up in inquiries.

As they rounded a curve in the quiet, tree-lined street, John raised a thumb and said, 'This'll do you. Pull over here. Leave the motor running. I'll pop the bag in and come straight back. Usually I have a drink or two with your man, but I'll make my excuses tonight. No need for him to see you lot and start asking questions.'

As Bliss pulled to the kerb, Paul surprised him by reacting. 'But you told me you'd introduce me this time,' he said to John. 'I'm due. I've waited long enough.'

John threw open the door and reached down for the bag nestling between his feet in the footwell. He looked over his shoulder. 'Next time. I promise.'

'No, not next time. This time. It's what I'm owed.'

'Don't be a twat. You can see these are not the best circumstances. As it is, he'll wonder why I've not parked up the driveway as usual. He sees you with me and we make introductions, he'll start asking questions. I don't want to explain why I brought George and Ringo with us, and I'm not about to get caught up in any lies.'

While they were talking, Bliss was getting a look at the house beyond the brick and wrought-iron fencing. From this vantage point he could see little more than rooftops, but the place was massive, with multiple gables either side of a stone archway. From what he knew of the price range in this area, the pile had to be worth upward of four million pounds. Not oil tycoon wealth, but top notch for a villain.

Meanwhile, he wondered about the sting operation. Had everything gone according to plan, this area would now be surrounded. Somebody would have eyes on, allowing John time enough to reach the house and hand the diamonds over to his paymaster. At that point, the watching teams would pounce. Fast, loud, and heavy.

Bliss's attention was snagged back by the squabbling between John and Paul, an echo perhaps of the massive clash of egos between the two real Beatles. Their voices were raised now, Paul not backing down. This felt like the right time to intervene.

'This is getting us nowhere,' he said. His voice was calm, but loud enough to slice through the thickening tension inside the car. 'Are either of you willing to listen to suggestions?'

John glanced across at him, raising his chin. 'You're full of bright ideas today, aren't you, Georgie boy? Go on, then. What's the latest?'

'Obviously I don't know who we're dealing with here, but I have to assume he's no dummy. Intelligent enough to ask himself why you would leave the motor out here on the street, irrespective of what you tell him. You know the man and I don't, but I reckon there's every chance of that niggling him more than the truth. It might make him doubt your sincerity, which in turn might make him question whether he can trust you.'

'And your answer is..?' Paul asked. He didn't say a great deal, but Bliss always had the impression there was more going on inside his head.

'We give him precisely that. I drive in and park up outside his front door like John would've. All you two have to do is explain what happened: that the second motor wouldn't start, so you had no option but to have me drive you out here. He might be pissed off with you for a moment, but at least that way he'll have no lingering suspicions.'

Both men thought it over. Ringo kept his tongue, not willing to get involved. Bliss wet his lips, taking deliberate shallow breaths. It was all he could do to fight off the adrenaline surge at the thought of what was about to take place.

Eventually, John conceded the point. He pulled the door closed and turned in his seat to face forward once more. 'George, take us inside. You and Ringo stay in the car. Paul, you come to the front door with me.'

Bliss let his breath go in a long, silent gasp of pent-up air. His plan had taken several knock-backs, as strategies do when they encounter an unanticipated barrier. But now it was back on track, and all that was left was for his boss to give the word to strike.

If they were out there, that is. If they had caught on quickly to the location change and followed him all the way here. Bliss didn't know what might happen next if they hadn't, and he had no desire to find out.

TWENTY-FOUR

F THE ENTRANCE AND driveway was impressive, the
property itself was breathtaking. With an architec-
tural design all of its own, its three storeys reached out
towards the clouds and it seemed to go on forever. Its
hulking stone façade reminded Bliss of a castle fortress,
and all that was lacking was a moat, its drawbridge
down and waiting for their arrival.

Before John and Paul had exited the vehicle, one of
the two vast front doors to the house was pulled open.
The man who stood there in the entrance was somebody Bliss instantly recognised. When Ringo uttered,
'Fuck me!' from the rear seat, he knew the young fireman also knew the man whose plan this heist had been.

Edward Frost ran a business empire ranging from
upmarket international stores and hotels, to owner-
ship of a football club, from holding onto the reins of a

major bank, to running a successful record label. There were few financial pies into which he had not deposited a finger, and yet here he was masterminding the theft of uncut diamonds whose net worth probably wouldn't come close to what he already had.

Bliss had heard of his type before. Men who seemingly had everything, and so yearned for more, risking everything on shady deals and associating with shabby people. Men who were as comfortable at Buckingham Palace collecting gongs as they were visiting Charlie Chan's nightclub at the Walthamstow greyhound stadium. Men who lived close to the edge, with absolutely everything to play for.

Frost looked at ease inside his own skin. A tall man who carried himself well, he had not allowed middle age to soften his rough edges. Bliss knew his reputation as a Wapping boy done good, the entrepreneurial son of a Smithfields meat market porter. Bliss regarded him and wondered how much of his wealth had been harvested from the sweat, toil and blood served up by the criminal underclass.

As Frost, John and Paul spoke, Bliss struggled to hear their indistinct and muffled conversation. He sensed in the odd gesture that their discussion was strained, and at one point, Frost's gaze flitted across towards the car and the two men still sitting inside. For a moment, Bliss felt his eyes lock with the supposed pillar of the community. The man said something to John, who glanced over his shoulder before shaking his head and responding to what Bliss assumed had been a question.

Who are these two men?

Followed by the unasked question: *can they be trusted?*

Bliss felt his lips thinning. *Not me you can't*, he thought. *I'm the man who is about to bring everything crashing down around your ears.*

His real colleagues were supposed to approach initially using blues but no twos, meaning lights flashing but without the usual accompanying sirens. In this way they would surround the entire property with specialist takedown teams, plus armed officers from the Met's PT17 armed unit scattered around at critical points both inside and outside the grounds. During the planning stage, it was Bliss who had recommended all vehicles cut their flashing lights as they neared the property, to give as little warning as possible.

So when Bliss caught a familiar flickering on the periphery of his vision, he immediately knew somebody had cocked up. Though the vehicle itself was not directly visible, its lights were caught in multiple reflections on trees running along the neighbouring street it was travelling. Bliss checked his mirror and could tell Ringo had not yet noticed them. But when he looked back at the three men gathered together by the door-way, it was obvious they had.

Several things happened at the same time. Frost dropped the bag he'd been given and stepped back inside the house, slamming the door on both John and Paul. Ringo swore as he now also reacted. Bliss went along with it, but inside his heart seemed to grow steel claws which scraped at the outer edges of his ribs. He thought furiously, and what came to mind first was the shotgun.

By now, John and Paul had turned on their heels and were dashing back to the car. But Bliss clambered out and raced around to the back, yanking open the boot.

'What the fuck are you doing!?' John yelled at him. 'Get us out of here.'

'I'm fetching the shooter,' Bliss called out, injecting panic into his voice. It didn't require any acting ability on his part.

'We ain't got time!' John was by his side now, grabbing hold of his arm.

Bliss glared at the man. 'And without it we don't stand a chance.'

'Fuck! I'll grab it, you get her started.'

His initial alarm swelling to the point of bursting, Bliss knew he had to prevent John from reaching the weapon first. The two men buried their hands deeper into the boot, scrambling around beneath the large bags laden with jewellery, reaching for the sawn-off which lay wedged between one of the holdalls and the tool box. They fought for the same few inches of space, before both looked up at the sound of engines racing, growing louder.

'Leave it, leave it!' John cried, 'Just get going!'

Bliss felt himself starting to sweat. If he jumped back into the car now, he would no longer be in control of the situation. But if he couldn't lay his hands on the shotgun, at least John wouldn't have use of it, either. He looked over the boot lid at the big man who happened to glance up at the same time. Their eyes met, and Bliss knew that John recognised his hesitation.

The two seemed to grasp the shotgun at precisely the same moment. They wrestled for the weapon, grunting and gasping as they took it in turns to gain the upper hand. After a few seconds came the inevitable: the shotgun went off.

Bliss reacted violently as a tongue of flame licked the side of his face. He was forced back a step, which loosened his grip on the gun. A high-pitched screech filling his ears, Bliss staggered, feeling for his face, wondering when the pain was going to come flooding in. John stared at him for a moment that seemed to freeze time, but as Bliss continued to shuffle away he also raised a hand and dangled the car keys from his fingers. Enraged, John let out a roar of undiluted anger and pain at being played.

Movement came from all sides now. Tyres slewed on loose stones. Muted shouts and cries of warning echoed around the grounds. His legs weakening, Bliss felt the stinging jolt of defeat. He realised he had not been shot during the first blast, but now stared down the barrel with one live cartridge still locked and loaded.

'You're a wrongun,' John snarled, his face twisted with bitterness and spite. 'I knew it, you wee bastard! I could smell it on you.' He hefted the shotgun and took aim down the shortened barrel.

Bliss could only stare back in horror. *I'm sorry, Hazel. I let you down. Always know that I loved you, sweetheart. I'm so sorry I won't be coming home.*

By this time, Paul had climbed out of the Beemer. He calmly walked around and moved to John's side. 'Here,' he said, holding out his hands. 'Let me do the wanker. Frost will be looking on. Taking this fucker out will earn me points while I'm doing a stretch inside, and you won't be charged with murder.'

A huge grin creasing his face, John handed over the weapon without a word. Bliss understood he had no time to move out of range. Paul took a step closer. He raised the shotgun to eye level. Then he winked at Bliss and swivelled, the barrels now aimed directly at John's head.

'You're done, Declan,' he said. But he did not fire. Instead, he continued speaking. 'You are nicked, old son.'

TWENTY-FIVE

BLISS LOOKED ON IN stunned silence as Billy Knowles and Declan O'Shea were cuffed and arrested, both men covered by armed officers at all times. Not that the constant whine in his ears allowed him too much quiet within that silence. The shotgun blast had taken place so close to his head that his hearing would be muffled for days.

The arrests made, Paul sauntered over to him, hands buried deep into his trouser pockets. His grin was that of a cat who had enjoyed several bottles of cream. 'You did well,' he said. 'I didn't know you were one of us until I had your gaff turned over the other night.'

'You had someone break into my flat?' Bliss felt his shoulders sag as he sighed. 'I thought it had to be Declan.'

'Nah. He had his suspicions about you, but nothing he could put his finger on. I offered to check it out for him.'

'So why the fuck did you have me choked out?'

'Yeah, sorry about that. It wasn't part of the plan, but my colleague had to make it look good, and I couldn't have you knowing about me.'

'How long have you been under?'

'Not far off a year.'

'And you've not been able to pinch Declan before now?'

'O'Shea was never our ultimate target.' Paul held out a hand. 'My name isn't Roy Gilbert, either. It's Adrian Fry. Detective Sergeant with the Flying Squad.'

The two men completed a firm handshake. 'The Sweeney, eh? I'm impressed. I suppose by now you already know I'm DC Jimmy Bliss. So, I'm guessing you were after Frost?'

The DS nodded. 'Although we didn't know it until today. We've been interested in the O'Shea brothers for a while now, but we always had the sense they were the tip of the iceberg. I went under in order to get close to Declan, earn his trust to first do jobs with him, and then get an introduction to the man pulling the strings. Tonight, as you overheard in the car, was my introductory night. I was hooked up with a wire and had to get that meeting.'

'I did wonder why you pushed him so hard. Oh, and thanks. You know, for stepping in and saving my arse. You took a risk grabbing that shooter off Declan. It's a wonder you weren't put down yourself.'

'Not really. PT17 were advised prior to leaving their base not to target either of us.'

Shaking his head, Bliss said, 'So how did you know about me? I swear my flat was spotless.'

Fry opened his mouth, then seemed to change his mind about what to say. 'Think about it, Jimmy. You actually nailed it perfectly.'

It took a second or two, but he got there. 'Oh. Right. I said my gaff was spotless. It was too clean, yeah?'

'Exactly. Take a tip from me: if you are playing the role of a young, single villain with time on his hands and cash on the hip, you have to live like one. A few dirty films, a bit of swag, some knock-offs. You'd have the best of things, nothing average. As for your clobber... it was your gear that first raised questions in my own head. You need better clothes next time. Make sure your skipper weighs in with a larger budget.'

Bliss puffed out his lips. 'I'm not sure if there'll be a next time. This didn't exactly go according to plan.'

Fry shrugged. 'They never do, pal. It's not expected. What sorts the wheat from the chaff, Jimmy, is how you react. You got lucky with that safe, but you handled things well when it looked as if Declan might turn nasty. I'll make sure people know about that.'

'Cheers. So, who from my own team knew you were also under?'

'Everybody. After I sussed you, I had to report it to my boss. He dug around, came up with the sting you lot were pulling. First thing they wondered was if we should all opt out, but eventually it was decided that we were too deep to pull back at such a late stage. I told them I'd keep an eye on you.'

'Why did nobody tell me?'

'That was my doing. I found out this was your first time working undercover. My concern was that you'd act differently if you knew about me. I had to have you treat me the same way as you'd been doing all along. To at least see how it worked out. Better that than pull the plug. I was too invested, to be honest.'

Bliss thought about how close he had come to being blasted with the shotgun. He mentioned it to Fry, who blew out a deep breath. 'Yeah, I have to admit my 'arris was puckering at that point. To be straight with you, Jimmy, I didn't think you had it in you to tussle with the big man, and especially not over a bleedin' shotgun cocked and ready to fire. Scared the crap out of me when it went off.'

'Yeah. Didn't do my underwear any favours, either. Plus, you're a foot away and I can barely hear you.'

Fry nodded and slapped him on the back. 'It's always a result when you can walk away, Jimmy. This is a bloody good collar for your first job as a DC, and my report ain't exactly going to hurt your reputation. I don't say this to many people, but if the time came around again, I'd be happy to work alongside you.'

'You, too. By the way, I have to ask about the limp. Is that real or affected as part of your cover?'

'It's real, but exaggerated. No big deal, but if you've got it, flaunt it, right?'

Bliss nodded. He decided he liked this man. 'Absolutely. And by the way, the first time I knew you were a copper was the day I met you.'

'You what?'

Bliss laughed. 'No, not really. You had me fooled right up until you turned the gun on O'Shea. Nice working with you, Sergeant.'

'You, too, Constable. From what I saw during this op, you've got a great career ahead of you. You never know, I might be calling you sir one of these days.'

The two men shook hands again and started to walk across to where their own units were now gathered, directly outside Frost's front door, the man himself having been arrested and spirited away along with the Irishman and the fireman. Bliss felt bad for Billy Knowles. He was a decent bloke, had no harm in him from what Bliss could tell. He simply couldn't survive on a fireman's salary and got a bit too greedy.

Bliss looked up at the mansion-style house looming over them. Talk about greed…

TWENTY-SIX

WELL PAST MIDNIGHT. ELSEWHERE in the hospital, visitors had long since been ushered out of cubicles, rooms and wards so that staff could perform their final duties of the day. The corridors were largely empty, though the echo of Bliss's footsteps made it sound as if any number of people were following him.

The psychiatric ward tended to work to slightly different hours, offering a little more flexibility to friends and relatives of the mentally ill. Bliss was neither friend nor relative, yet he found himself there all the same. He had not been able to let go. Unescorted and unchallenged, he made his way to Angie Borthwick's room. Its door was wedged open, lights switched off, but the fierce glow of a full moon was bright enough to illuminate his way.

The woman who had occupied his thoughts since the conclusion of the undercover operation was asleep. Tonight her hair was clean. Thicker. It had a warm lustre as it coiled around her neck. She wore a pale blue nightdress, drawstrings fastened in a bow beneath her throat. She looked at peace, which made Bliss smile for the first time in what felt like a long while.

Though still sedated, Angie was moving ever closer to returning to the world beyond the hospital walls. Bliss couldn't help but wonder what that first experience of entering her own home and, in particular, Michael's room, might do to her. The effect could be powerful enough to send her fragile mind reeling all over again. Hers was clearly a guilt so profound it might well find a way to torment the poor woman for the rest of whatever remained of her natural life.

Bliss stood looking down at Michael's mother for a good fifteen minutes. She did not wake, and he was glad of it. He could think of nothing to say to her that would improve her life. But before he left, he took a step closer to the bed and placed in the crook of her left arm the object he had brought with him. The moment the soft toy touched her flesh, Angie reflexively drew it closer and held on to it as if it were her child.

'She's going to need you,' Bliss whispered to Baloo the bear. 'Be strong for her.'

And with that, he slipped quietly away.

TWENTY-SEVEN

THE WEEKEND WAS PRACTICALLY over before Bliss felt able to tell his parents and Hazel what he'd been up to for the past few weeks. He had spent most of Saturday attending various briefings and post-op inquiries, writing up reports, and in less formal discussions with a whole range of people.

He'd received congratulations and warm handshakes from everybody except DI Moody. 'I suppose you think you're the absolute dog's bollocks now,' he'd said to Bliss when they were alone in the Inspector's office. He stood by the window, hands in pockets, legs spread wide, feet splayed. 'Well think again, *Constable*. You seem to have everyone else here fooled, but not me. They might see sunshine blazing out of your ringpiece, but don't expect me to put on my sunglasses anytime soon.'

'Thank you, sir,' Bliss had responded.

Moody's brow creased. 'For what?'

'For living down to my low expectations. You had a chance to show a bit of class. I took bets on it. I'm quids in.'

Moody had leaned forward, fists resting on the desk, white knuckles supporting his weight. 'Do you really want to make an enemy of me, son?'

'It's too late for that, Guv. You already made that decision for me.'

It wasn't his finest moment, but Bliss had gone into the day on the back of no sleep. His mind had been a whirl of jumbled thoughts and images, and every time he closed his eyes those visions grew darker and more violent. One that repeated itself time and again was his struggle over the shotgun with Declan O'Shea. As they'd fought for control, O'Shea's already sizeable figure grew taller and more broad, like some cartoon character swelling to the point of bursting. The man laughed throughout, his massive shoulders heaving and both eyes bulging. Then, with the Irishman scream-ing hysterically, the gun went off. All at once, Bliss was watching himself from a distance, spinning like a top, arms flapping around wildly, his head missing and his neck spurting blood like a derrick gushing crude oil.

He knew how lucky he was. How close he had come to not making it home. The scorch marks and debris from the blast had turned one side of his face both red and black. He'd been given some medicated ointment for it to prevent infection. He brushed aside people's questions until he felt emotionally stable enough to talk about it.

Throughout Saturday and Sunday morning, Bliss sought a more secluded spot in which to replay those events. Hazel and his parents left him to it, something for which he was truly grateful. The fact that the undercover operation and ultimate sting had been successful was merely one part of the equation. The other was how he had carried himself. Allowances would be made for how callow he was in terms of experience when it came to working undercover. He could be his own worst critic, but when he reflected back over the entire job, he thought he had done well enough not to be embarrassed about his performance.

Which was precisely what he told everybody after Sunday dinner, Hazel curled up with him on the sofa, his parents in their favourite chairs. Some Gregory Peck and David Niven film was on in the background. Bliss focussed on delivering what he had to say. His mother gasped and put a hand to her mouth when he mentioned the break-in at his supposed safe house flat. So much so that he glossed over the shotgun incidents, keeping details to a minimum and making it seem as if he was never in any real danger. His face told a somewhat different story, however.

Bliss's father sat stoically throughout, nodding occasionally, taking it all in without reacting with any emotion. Not that Jimmy wanted any from him. Knowing his father, he'd be calculating the potential effect on his son's career, rather than dwelling on what was already shrinking into the past. It was how Bliss himself preferred to think of it, but he had wanted to clear the air so that those closest to him would understand any unwarranted or strange behaviour he might display in the coming days.

His story finished, Bliss felt Hazel's arms tighten around him. His mother reacted by making tea, and he knew she would shed a tear or two in the kitchen. His father gave it a little more thought before voicing his opinion.

'I think they were wrong to come to you so soon with this, Jimmy, but it sounds to me as if you pulled it off. Flying colours, too. Like I told you when you started this job, coming home at the end of each shift is the only thing that counts. You'll have earned yourself some respect, but you also broke the cardinal rule.'

Bliss was surprised. 'Which is?'

'Never to volunteer for anything.'

'But I didn't. They came to me.'

'I don't mean the job. You came up with a change to their original plan. That's the same thing as volunteering in my book.'

He understood what his father meant, and agreed. But this was one of those times when their differences shone through. 'Thing is, dad, I thought it was the better option. You've taught me a lot down the years, but the one early lesson I remember most is to do the right thing as often as you can. Improving the plan was the right thing to do.'

'Maybe you could have waited until someone else came up with it. Let them put their head on the chopping block.'

'It hadn't happened up until that point. I thought it, I suggested it. I still think it was the best outcome for the sting.'

Dennis Bliss heaved himself up out of his armchair. 'I'd best help your mother,' he said. When he reached the living room door he stopped, paused in place for a moment, then turned. 'I stand by my advice never to volunteer, but I know that when it's the right thing to do, you'll do it. Always. That's just who you are, son.' He smiled and nodded. 'Don't ever lose that. Not like I did.'

Hazel's mouth was hanging open when Bliss turned to look at her. 'I know,' he said. 'For my old man, that was a speech and a half. That was him bubbling over.'

'He's proud of you. That's what he was actually saying.'

'You think?'

She sighed. 'If only you men could talk and say the actual words you mean without getting all silly about it. There'd be no need for women to interpret on your behalf.'

Bliss grinned. 'What he did say was enough for me. There's no need to get all sloppy about it.'

Hazel hugged him tight. 'No, save all that for me, eh?'

'I'll be as sloppy as you like when we're on our own.'

She snuggled into him. 'Which reminds me... I thought we might go out later and perhaps end up at my place. I have some sexy black underwear in need of putting on and ripping off again.'

'I'll drink my tea quickly.'

'Sod that. Pour it into the plant pot. I'm going to treat you for coming home safe.'

Bliss locked eyes with the woman he loved. 'I'm always doing that, Haze,' he said. 'Every single day for the rest of my life.'

'It's going to be a great life, Jimmy. You and me, I mean. Together.'

'Yeah. The best.'

'How long do you think we have? Forty years? Fifty?'

'Easily.' Bliss ducked lower to kiss Hazel's lips. 'Either way, it's nowhere near enough.'

ACKNOWLEDGEMENTS

T HOSE WHO HELPED ME with this know who you are. I'm sure you'd rather bask in your anonymity than see your name spread all over here again, right? Hmm... maybe not. Please send all complaints to tonyforder. not@thisaddress.com.

Actually, I do need to mention one person in particular. My fellow author, friend and great supporter, Maggie James, virtually turned her ARC read of this into an edit and proofing session, and in doing so came up with some great suggestions that helped to improve the story. I said I would send her something moist and bloody for her trouble, and if anyone deserves such a gift, it's her.

Anyway, writing this was great fun. And so much more than a folly. I wanted a way to show my readers an earlier version of Jimmy Bliss. A Bliss minus his team, especially the Penny Chandler rock to whom he clings so precariously at times. I wanted readers to get to know Jimmy's parents just a little, and to meet Hazel – the woman who haunts his dreams still. These people helped shape the man Bliss is.

This is a brash, even a little bit cocky version of Bliss, yet hopefully you will recognise his insecurities behind the front he throws up. Throughout this novella I scattered tiny little precursors to the Jimmy Bliss you have become familiar with. I hope you spotted them all.

Bliss Uncovered is a quick story, told within the limitations of a novella. I felt that it was a good way to introduce you to Jimmy's past, without going for the full novel – I confess, I am not a huge fan of series books that provide lengthy prequels. I'm not adverse to doing more of these, but the story would have to hold up on its own. For now, I'm content with having shown you this glimpse into the past, and hope you found it as interesting as I did.

Finally… we all know that 2020 has been a shit year for so many people in so many ways. None of us can peer into the future, so all I can do is wish you all a better 2021 and for you to be of good health and cheer.

Jimmy Bliss will be back in 2021 with *The Autumn Tree*.

Take care and be safe.
Tony

Printed in Great Britain
by Amazon

47002792R00118